WILD ACE

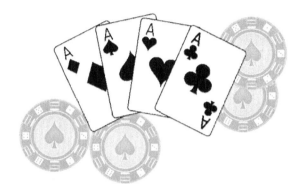

CARFANO CRIME FAMILY
BOOK 5

REBECCA GANNON

newsletter, blog, shop, and links to all social media:
www.rebeccagannon.com

More by Rebecca Gannon

Pine Cove
Her Maine Attraction
Her Maine Reaction
Her Maine Risk
Her Maine Distraction

Carfano Crime Family
Casino King
The Boss
Vengeance
Executioner
Wild Ace

Standalone Novels
Whiskey & Wine
Redeeming His Reputation

To those who don't know if they should take that chance that might change their lives, take it.
Gamble. Win. Love.

THE CARFANO FAMILY

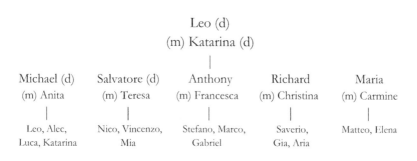

Leo (d)
(m) Katarina (d)

Michael (d)	Salvatore (d)	Anthony	Richard	Maria
(m) Anita	(m) Teresa	(m) Francesca	(m) Christina	(m) Carmine
Leo, Alec, Luca, Katarina	Nico, Vincenzo, Mia	Stefano, Marco, Gabriel	Saverio, Gia, Aria	Matteo, Elena

(m) – married / (d) – deceased

"She's not mine yet
I don't think you can belong to someone
Anymore
But how I would love her
If she could be mine"

- Courtney Peppernell
"Pillow Thoughts III"

CHAPTER 1

Lexi

My nonno sighs and takes his glasses off, rubbing the bridge of his nose. "You need to go out more, Alexis."

Smiling, I shake my head. "I go out."

"If you mean you leave your apartment to come here to check on me before and after your classes to make sure I'm okay, then yes, you go out."

A small laugh bubbles out of me. "Nonno!"

"Alexis, honey, you're young. You need to go out and have fun. Meet a man."

"I have time for all of that."

"Not as much as you think. One day you'll wake up old like me and realize you should've done a lot more when you were young."

"You're not old, nonno, and you know I love you and this place."

Four months ago, he tore his ACL after a misstep he had walking down the stairs from his apartment above the deli. He's owned and operated Manzato's Delicatessen for forty years and has walked those stairs thousands of times over the decades, but with one slip, I'm reminded that one of the only family members I have left isn't as young as I think he is.

I had only just started my fall semester of my senior year of college when it happened, so I was able to drop all my classes without penalty to take care of him and make sure the deli remained open and operating. But on his insistence, I started school again for the spring semester two weeks ago and he hired a local boy to pick up some of the slack.

"I know, but it's Friday and I don't need your help for the rest of the day. So, I'm demanding you take the rest of it off from checking up on me. Tomorrow, too. Call that friend of yours from school who came by the other week to say hi and go out and have fun tonight."

"I don't think—"

"I insist," he says, cutting me off. "Now go." He starts pushing me towards the door.

"Nonno!"

"Go! Go! Dress up and have fun!"

"Alright!" I laugh. "I'm going. But I make no promises about tomorrow."

"We'll see," he mumbles, and I smile as I'm shuffled out the door.

I spent so much of my childhood in that deli, loving that it had my last name loud and proud on the wooden sign above the awning. Both are faded and weathered now, and in need of replacing, but it's still there, and I'm still proud.

My nonno and nonna came over from Italy almost fifty years ago. She was the daughter of a wealthy vineyard owner and he worked in the fields. They got married in secret when they found out she was pregnant and after her father threatened my nonno for trying to steal his daughter away when she was meant for someone better. And by better, he meant richer.

They chose to sever all ties and ran away to America to start a new life together, making sure both them and their baby, my father, were given a chance at a happy life away from my nonna's controlling family.

They settled in Atlantic City and rented the apartment above the deli where my nonno got a job. It was called Sunrise Deli before, but when my nonno took over, he renamed it.

He built a life for him and my nonna that they enjoyed together for many years until my nonna passed away five years ago. My father passed away five years before she did, and since they couldn't have any more children after my father due to complications, the only family I'm left with is my nonno and my mom. Although, my mom has been in New York City with her new husband for a few years, living her second act in life, so it's just my nonno and I in this city I've called home my entire life.

The deli has always been my second home, and it's been

hard to see it fall into the state it has, having had little to no updates or renovations over the past four or five decades. That hasn't kept the devoted regulars away, though. They know the quality of food is far above anything else in town, and my nonno is one-of-a-kind and a friend to all. He knows every single one of his regular's names, and makes a point to get to know each and every one of his returning customers. He always said a customer should only be a customer once, after that, they're a friend.

I love him for that.

He's the kindest man I know. He's the best man I know. Which is why I'd do anything to help him. Put college on hold, go to work with him every day, take care of him to make sure he has everything he needs. Anything. But he's right, I do need to make a little more room in my life for fun.

Getting in my car, I pull out my phone to call my best friend. I'm not a big fan of this car. Every time I'm in it, it reminds me that my mom's new husband bought it for me because my previous one finally broke down right after they got married, and he insisted. I knew he was just being nice and trying to help me, so I let him. But that doesn't mean I don't wish I didn't.

He's a nice enough guy, and he treats my mom well, but he's not my dad.

My parents were both dealers at Sahara's Casino, which is how they met. But about six years ago, four years after my dad died, Charles became a regular at my mom's poker table. Every time he was in town from the city, he would only ever sit at her table, talking to her between games and always trying to get her to go out with him after her shift.

My mom is gorgeous, smart, and doesn't take shit from anyone, which is how she liked to tell me she won my dad over. He loved that she was a strong woman who liked to live life to the fullest. So, it's no wonder the rich, handsome, and successful businessman from New York City was drawn to her and pursued her until she finally agreed to go out with him.

She turned him down for a few years, I think in part to me still being in high school at the time and not wanting to do anything that might change my life before I was able to be on my own. But I also think it was in part to her being scared to move on with her life after my dad.

I knew she would eventually, and I really do want her to be happy, but I still miss my dad.

Pulling up my text thread with my friend Cassie, I tap the call button, and it only takes two rings for her to answer.

"Hey, Lex," she greets.

"Hey, are you busy tonight?"

"I am now," she says, and I can hear the excitement in her voice. "What are we doing?"

"My grandfather just threw me out of the deli and ordered me to call you to get dressed up and go out."

"Your grandpa is amazing." She laughs. "And since he ordered you to, that means we have to."

"Exactly."

I met Cassie on my first day of classes freshman year of college. She came breezing in five minutes late and took the empty seat beside me, ignoring the look the professor was giving her. Instead, she whispered hi to me and took a sip of her iced coffee that I later found out was the reason she was late. That's when I knew we would be good friends.

"I've been *dying* to go to Royals, the club inside The Aces Casino, since I turned 21. These girls in class last week were talking way too loud about it, bragging about how amazing it was."

I roll my eyes. "Of course they were. Want to come over and get ready together? I'm leaving the deli now."

"Yes, I'm looking through my closet as we speak. Oh!" she gasps. "I'm bringing this for you to wear. It's going to look amazing and show off everything that needs showing off!"

"I have clothes, Cass."

"But not this dress. See you soon!" She hangs up before I can say anything else and I shake my head, already knowing it's going to be an adventurous night.

It's only a five-minute drive to my apartment, and once inside, I clean up a little, pull out takeout menus for options while we get ready, and pour the rest of my open bottle of wine into a glass to down before Cassie gets here.

I haven't gone out dancing or drinking since before my nonno's fall, and now that he's forced it on me, I'm actually pretty excited. That doesn't mean I won't step out at some point to call him to make sure he's okay, though.

Her knock at the door comes a half hour later, and when I open it, she bursts in like the ball of human energy she is.

"I'm so glad you called me today," she says in a rush. "I've been dying to go out, but I know you're busy and it hasn't really been on your radar."

"Sorry, I—"

"No, I'm sorry," she says over me. "I didn't mean it negatively. I totally understand why. I've just missed you is all."

"Cassie," I croon, pulling her in for a hug. "I've missed you, too. I only have my grandfather and my mom now, and I just can't fathom losing him yet."

"You won't," she assures me. "He's doing well since the surgery, yes?"

"Yeah, which is why I should worry a little less, I guess."

"Exactly. And especially tonight. Tonight is about letting loose and having fun."

"I can get behind that." I smile.

"Then let's do a shot to seal the deal!" Cassie claps her hands together and goes to my freezer, knowing I always have a bottle of vodka at the ready.

She pulls out two short tumbler glasses from my cabinet and pours a good amount in each.

"That's more than a shot."

She smiles and shrugs, handing me one of the glasses. "It's a party shot."

Laughing, I clink glasses with hers and we shoot back our shots, the cold vodka going down easy.

"Just like old times," Cassie says with a wide grin. She looks down at the takeout menus I have on the counter and picks up the one for Anthony's Pizzeria. "Now, let's have one more shot for good measure, order a pizza, and then I'll show you the dress I brought for you."

I take this shot with a little more urgency than the last, knowing the dress she brought me will undoubtedly require me to have a little extra liquor to wear. I love Cassie for her confidence and love of clothes that show off her amazing curves, but I'm more reserved when it comes to showing off what my mom blessed me with.

I order us a pizza and she runs over to her bag. "You're going to love this!" Unzipping her overnight bag, she pulls out a rolled-up dress, and when she holds it up, my eyes widen and my jaw slacks.

"You can't be serious, Cass. That would barely cover me. Anywhere. I can't wear that. It's either boobs or legs, not both."

"Fine," she sighs. "I thought you'd say that, so I brought another one I think you'll like better." She pulls out another rolled up dress and holds it up.

I smile immediately, taking it from her. "Now that, I'll wear."

"I thought you'd say that. Which is why I showed you the other one first. It's the dress I'm going to wear." She smirks, grabbing her makeup bag and walking down the hall to my bathroom.

The dress is a pale pink bodycon with skinny spaghetti straps. It'll probably hit me mid-thigh, but the slit that goes up the entire thigh will show off some serious leg. Which is why I'm glad the straight-cut neckline will contain my boobs nicely.

Meeting Cassie in the bathroom, we do our hair together and then take a pizza break when it arrives before starting our makeup and slipping into our dresses.

"Damn, we look good," Cassie states matter-of-factly, turning to the left and right to look at herself from all sides. Her red hair is curled in big waves and it stands out nicely against her black dress. Her hair is like a siren to men. It never fails. "We're definitely going to have the men clamoring to buy us drinks tonight."

"I guess that would save me some money." I laugh, pulling my dress down at the hem and then up at the neckline.

"We have to think economically, Lex. But you know my rule. Neither of us leaves the other alone for anything or anyone. We can lure the men in, but we don't go anywhere alone with them."

We had a scary mishap back when we were freshman at a frat party that could've had a horrible ending had I not gone looking for her when she didn't come back from the bathroom after a while.

"I know," I say reverently, and we share a look.

"Just making sure." Clearing her throat, she gives herself one more look in the mirror and then leaves to go put her heels on.

I follow her into my room and do the same. "I haven't worn heels in a long time. I'm not looking forward to the pain I'm going to endure in a few hours."

"Don't worry, we'll just numb it with liquor. Or maybe find a way to weasel ourselves into VIP so we can sit."

"Sounds good." I smile.

Transferring my essentials into my small purse, I order us a cab.

CHAPTER 2

Lexi

The ride to The Aces is only ten minutes, and when we arrive, I instantly feel at ease inside the casino.

I've only legally been able to gamble on a casino floor for six months, but I've been gambling in casinos since I was eighteen and could pass as 'old enough'. Besides, gambling is a relative term to me because it insinuates a risk, and I don't risk much when I play. I win.

I haven't had to use my particular skill in a while, but when I did, I always made sure to stay under the five thousand earnings limit so I wouldn't have to show my ID and be outed as a minor, or fill out a form to claim my winnings as taxable income. I also flew under all the casinos' radars when it came to card counting by only winning in small batches and moving on, and then not returning for at least a month.

I went to a different casino almost every weekend, and never once had been stopped or questioned. I was good. I am good. I just haven't had to do it lately because I used my refund from my fall semester to pay for my spring semester, and I had a large enough stash of extra cash to live off of comfortably for a while.

On top of that, Charles bought out the apartment I live in when he first got together with my mom. He wanted to take a burden off her shoulders, which now means I get to live rent-free for as long as I'd like.

And while I'm very comfortable in the casinos in town, The Aces is the one I don't run my game on, knowing full-well it's run by the Carfano family. My mom told me to be careful if I ever went there. She said the Carfanos weren't to be underestimated or messed with. Ever.

Of course, that only made me want to go more, and when I finally did, it was quite underwhelming. I don't know why I thought I would be bumping into real-life mafia men the moment I walked inside. I was picturing overweight Italian men standing guard, each with a fat cigar in one hand and a pinkie ring on his other as he runs it through his thinning hair. There were none in sight. Not even close.

I know the mafia doesn't always look like the Sopranos, so I could've been standing near a Carfano and didn't even know it. I still didn't run my game there, though, just to be safe.

As Cassie and I walk through the casino, we get looks from everyone we pass. And when the umpteenth man gives us the up and down look, Cassie and I smirk at each other.

"That just confirms we look amazing," she says.

We follow the signs that lead us around the entire casino to the line that has already formed to get into their club, Royals.

"This is going to take forever to get in."

"I've been keeping a secret," Cassie says casually. "You know those annoying girls I said were talking loudly about how much fun they had here a few weeks ago?" I nod. "Well, I decided to join in the conversation once one mentioned that their cousin's boyfriend was one of the bouncers. I texted her after you called and she said she's going tonight too, and would give him our names to let us right in."

"You sneaky little minx."

"I know how to turn an annoying situation into something beneficial." Grabbing my hand, Cassie walks us past everyone in line and up to the bouncer. "Hey, Santiago."

"Hi, gorgeous, what can I do for you?"

"Jackie's waiting for us inside. She said she'd tell you I was coming. I'm Cassie, and this is my friend, Lexi."

"Yes, she did. But she failed to tell me how gorgeous you'd be."

"It's always better to be surprised," Cassie teases, and Santiago rubs his chin, looking her up and down.

"Yes, it is." His voice drops, and Cassie runs her fingers down his forearm as he unclips the velvet rope.

"Thank you."

"Have fun, ladies."

Cassie flashes him a smile. "Oh, we will." And when we walk out of earshot, she sarcastically says, "Wow, Jackie's cousin is a lucky girl."

We walk down a hallway that's lit only by small, dim lights lining the sides, and the thudding of music pulses through me – the beat and my heart pounding with every step closer to the source. There's another bouncer a short distance ahead who pulls back a thick black curtain, causing the music to hit me square in the chest.

We're at the top of a large staircase and I look down at everyone below, my anxiety spiking at the thought of being around so many people after not going out for so long. But I breathe through it, and by the time we reach the bottom, my head is clear and my pulse is back in tempo with the music.

"I've got the first round," I tell Cassie, and the men around the bar don't even hesitate to part for us.

It doesn't take long for us to get our drinks, and since I can't dance before I have at least a few in me, we stand at a high-top table near the bar that was just vacated by a group of girls. I'm not ready to flirt for drinks yet, either.

"So, I've been trying to date recently," Cassie says loud enough for me to hear over the music.

"Wait, seriously?" I ask, surprised.

"Yeah," she sighs, rolling her eyes. "I downloaded a stupid app and have gone on a date almost every weekend for two months now. It's annoying and it fucking sucks."

"Every weekend? That sounds exhausting."

"It has been. And get this, none of them were even

second or third dates. They were *all first dates*. It feels like all I've done is repeat myself over and over again to each guy, and they've all started to blur together. I'm telling you, I couldn't pick a single one out of a lineup if I was asked to."

"Dating isn't even on my radar right now," I tell her, taking a long sip of my drink. "And based on what you just told me, I'm glad it isn't."

"You need to get out there though, Lex. Let a man distract you from life."

"Who says I need a distraction?"

"I do. You need some fun in your life. You put school on hold to take care of your grandpa, and then went right back to school while still helping him as much as you can. You need something for yourself. And by that, I mean some dick. Some really great dick to make you black out in bliss for a while between it all."

"Cassie!" I yell, laughing loudly.

"What?"

"How about instead of talking about the lack of a man or men in my life, we go take a couple shots, get another drink, and then go out on the dance floor and see if our luck changes?"

She grins. "Sounds like the perfect plan."

We throw back two shots of tequila each, and the liquor pools warmly in my stomach, spreading to my limbs and head, loosening me up. Tequila was the first liquor I ever tried when I was in high school, and I've always found it to be the one that gets me drunk the quickest, and the one that makes me feel the best when I am.

With fresh drinks in hand, we make our way out onto the dance floor and my body moves to the music without thought. I get lost in my own world for a few songs until there's a tap on my shoulder.

I turn towards the source, annoyed at being snapped out of my trance. But when I'm met with a wall of a man who happens to be the most attractive man I've ever laid eyes on, my annoyance evaporates.

He's tall, dark, and handsome, standing at at least 6'2" or 3" with dark hair and eyes, a clean-shaven face that features a chiseled jawline, and tanned skin that looks like he just got back from a vacation in Italy. He's sure as hell not getting that color from Jersey in January.

My eyes roam over his face, neck, and chest, and my tongue darts out to lick my lips when I look too long at the small exposed patch of chest visible with the top buttons of his black shirt undone.

When my eyes finally find their way back up to his face, he's smiling, showing off a set of white teeth I wouldn't mind running my tongue over to feel how smooth they are.

I can tell I missed something he said by the way he's looking at me. "What?" I ask, knowing it's not nearly loud enough for him to hear me, but his eyes follow my lips.

Leaning in close, he doesn't touch me, but I catch a whiff of his rich scent as his lips come closer to my ear. He smells like leather, amber, and a hint of cigar smoke that I find is intoxicating me more than the drink in my hand.

"I asked if you would like to dance."

"Okay," I whisper back with a small nod, and his fingers

run down my arm until he reaches my hand. Holding it in his, he immediately spins me around so my back is to his front.

There's a fraction of space between us still that's charged with electricity, bouncing between him and I, trying to pull us together.

My hips rock to the music and he leans in close again. "I haven't been able to take my eyes off you from the moment you walked in."

Closing my eyes, I don't fight the pull any longer and lean back against him, my body fitting perfectly with his. In my heels, my ass is at the perfect height to be nestled between his hips, and I can feel how much he likes what I'm doing.

I haven't felt a man's touch or been this close to one in so long, that I've clearly forgotten how to behave when a small moan escapes my lips at the feel of his hard length at my backside.

But this man…

I know it's probably just the alcohol and his hotness throwing me for a loop, but I'm going to embrace it while I can.

His arm is banded across my stomach as he holds me against him, letting me feel every inch of his hard body from his thighs to his chest, and I'm glad he's holding me, because my legs are starting to turn to jelly.

When the song changes, he grabs my hand again and spins me around so I'm facing him. Snaking his arms around my waist, he leans down and presses his forehead to mine. We're in our own little bubble where all I see and feel is him with the music pounding between us, making me oblivious to everything else.

Reaching up, I wrap one arm around his neck, pressing my fingertips into him.

He runs his nose down mine, our breaths mixing with how close our mouths are. If I tilted my head up even just the slightest, I could easily kiss him. I know it would absolutely electrify me, but I can't. I'm loving this moment too much to make it more. Once it's more, then the illusion is broken.

His hand slides down my lower back to cup my ass, and I gasp, pressing myself closer to him. A low rumble leaves his chest and vibrates into me.

"Come upstairs with me," he says in my ear, his voice rough – like rocks tumbling in the break of waves that then turn smooth in an enticing offer. "To the VIP lounge."

My breathing quickens. "I don't know," I say back, my lips brushing his ear.

His grip on me tightens. "I promise to be good. Or bad, if you want me to be," he teases, swirling his tongue around the spot right below my ear, then planting a kiss there. "Please," he adds, and I pinch my eyes closed, biting back another moan.

"I came here with my friend."

"I know. She's dancing with my brother, Nico. I'm sure he's already asked her, too."

"What does going upstairs entail?" I ask, needing to know what he thinks is going to happen.

"It entails a private bar, couches, and whatever else you want to do. Talk, dance, and maybe let me taste those lips of yours that are calling to me, begging to be tasted."

Oh, sweet Jesus.

"And if not," he continues, "then I'll just wonder for the rest of my life if I missed out on the best kiss of my fucking life."

Oh, God.

"Okay," I agree without hesitation, and he kisses the same spot below my ear again before pulling away and getting his brother's attention. He nods upstairs, and his brother's eyes flit to mine. He flashes me a grin and then bends down to say something in Cassie's ear. She's quick to nod, but looks to me to make sure I'm okay with it, and I give her a reassuring nod.

My mystery man leads us through the crowd and I place my drink on the first table we pass, feeling the envious eyes of every woman around on me.

We walk back up the staircase, and at the top, there's another thick, black curtain to the right like the one we entered through, this one so well hidden in the shadows, I thought it was just the wall.

Two men stand guard on the opposite side, and both nod at the men Cassie and I are with in acknowledgement as we pass by.

The VIP area is large, with a crescent shaped balcony that overlooks the DJ's booth and the dance floor below. The lights are rigged up on the sides and along the top of the balcony awning shining out and down, so they don't make their way inside the VIP lounge, but we can see everything below, and it's too bright for anyone to see up here.

It's dimly lit, with a full bar in the back corner, and a variety of tables, chairs, and couches all around, with the area around the balcony railing free for dancing.

I'm guided over to the bar. "What are you having, *bambina?*"

"Oh, I'm not your baby," I tell him, and he looks surprised I knew what he said right away.

"*Cara mia.*" He smiles, but I shake my head at that sentiment, too. My nonno always called my nonna *cara mia.*

"Fine, *la mia piccola dea italiana che non sa quanto mi ha gettato sotto il suo incantesimo.*"

"I don't know what you just said," I admit, blinking, dazed from how sexy he just sounded with fluent Italian spilling from his lips. Lips I want to taste so damn badly to see if the Italian tastes as sweet as it sounded.

"I didn't think you would." He smirks. "So, tell me what you were having."

"Tequila on the rocks. Extra limes."

His eyebrows raise, and I love that I surprised him. "You heard the lady," he says to the bartender. "And I'll have my usual."

I look over at Cassie on one of the couches with Nico, and it looks like she's about to crawl onto his lap and devour him whole.

"So, are you going to tell me your name?" I ask, distracting myself from how much I would love to devour this man, too.

"Vinny. Vin. Vincenzo if you want to call out my full name when the time comes." He smirks with a wink, and my panties dampen at his confidence.

"Alright, Vinny. I don't think that last one will happen, but I'm glad to know the option is there."

His smile is instant and I'm blinded by how freaking good-looking he is. He could charm the panties off anyone, including myself if I'm not careful. And right now, I so don't want to be careful.

Our drinks are placed in front of us and I take the break in tension to squeeze my limes into my tequila and take a sip, loving the cool burn of it as it goes down. It's keeping me grounded.

"Are *you* going to tell me your name?" he asks.

I lift one shoulder in a small shrug. "I haven't decided yet. I don't just give my name out to every stranger I dance with."

"That's fair." He nods. "But I think what we did down there was more than dancing. You don't think I've earned it?"

"Not yet," I tease, sipping my drink. I don't know why, but I don't want to give him my name just yet. I don't want to make anything easy on him when it so easily could be, and probably has been most of his life with the way he looks.

"I'll just have to try harder, then," he says, and my stomach knots. I *really* want to know what him trying harder entails. "Where are you from?"

"Here."

"Atlantic City?"

"Yeah, I love this place. It's my city. My grandparents came over from Italy and settled here. It's where they put their roots down and where I grew, I guess. I haven't felt the need to leave. Plus, my grandfather owns a deli in town."

"Don't tell me it's Manzato's?"

"It is. You know it?"

"This is my city too, and I'm Italian. Of course I know it. They have my favorite sandwich of all time."

"Let me guess…the soppressata?"

"Yes!" He laughs, grinning. "Your grandfather won't tell me how he makes that spicy red pepper spread that's on it. How did you know?"

"It's my favorite, too."

His smile grows even wider. "Huh, well then, I might just be stopping by sooner than I thought for one. I've talked to your grandfather many times when I've been in. He's a good man."

The fact that he knows and likes my nonno does something to my chest, and I have the urge to rub the spot above my heart, but I hold back. "He is, and he loves talking to everyone who walks through his doors. You haven't been in a little while, though, have you? I would have remembered you."

"Do you work there?"

"I always helped out growing up, but I've been helping him more full-time for the past five months. He had a little fall in September and tore his ACL. He had to have surgery, so I put school on hold to help him until he was back on his feet."

"You just dropped everything to help him?"

"Well, yeah, he's family, and one of only two people I

have left to call family. I would do anything for him."

"Family is important to me, too." Vinny takes a sip of his amber liquid and something in his eyes shifts the longer I look in them.

"Yes, I see that. You and your brother are a team when you go out and hit on women in a club."

"Only when he comes down from the city." He winks. "And this isn't just a club. It's mine. This whole place is. My family's, that is. I run The Aces with my cousin."

I'm momentarily stunned, my drink mid-air to my mouth. "This is your club? This is your casino?"

His lips quirk up in a smirk and his gaze darkens. "It is." His lifts his glass to his lips and takes a long drink, with his tongue gliding over his bottom one to catch an escaped drop of whiskey.

He's a Carfano.

The Carfanos own this casino.

I definitely wasn't picturing a man like him when I thought I'd run into the mafia at The Aces. He's certainly not an old fat Italian man with slicked back hair, a cigar, and a pinky ring. I don't think he's even thirty yet. He's sexy as hell, but that doesn't mean I should get involved with him. In fact, it means I *really* shouldn't get involved with him. Even for a night. I can see myself liking him too much. Plus, the sexy mafia bad boy combination is one that spells trouble with a side of heartbreak.

"I should go," I tell him, placing my drink down on the bar and stepping away.

"Wait," he says, his hand capturing my wrist, halting me.

I look down at where his fingers are wrapped around me and then up into his eyes, feeling that current flowing between us again. "This isn't a good idea," I tell him, my words steeped in regret.

"You know who I am?" he asks pointedly, putting it all out there. I nod. "And that scares you? Knowing who I am?" His eyes turn guarded when I don't answer right away. "I can see that it does, but it shouldn't."

"I'm not afraid of you," I say after a beat, and I mean it. He hasn't done anything that has caused me to feel frightened or weary, and I'd like to keep it that way.

Vinny rubs his thumb back and forth against my inner wrist and my pulse quickens. "Prove it," he challenges, the look in his eyes turning mischievous. "Stay."

Everything in me wants to, but I need a second to breathe without inhaling his intoxicating scent that's clouding my decision-making skills.

Looking away, I clear my throat. "Is there a restroom up here?"

"Back corner." He nods to the area behind me, but still has a hold of my wrist.

"I need my arm," I whisper, and he hesitates, but then releases me – the warmth he provided suddenly gone, making me shiver.

I shake it off and turn to get Cassie's attention, but she's too wrapped up in Vinny's brother to feel my silent plea for her to look up so I can signal her to meet me in the bathroom.

Dammit.

I need to tell her who the man she's with is.

I need to tell her that these brothers are dangerous to get close to, even for a single night. And then I need her to tell me that it doesn't matter. That a night with them would be worth whatever comes after.

Fuck. I'm in trouble.

I take slow, deliberate steps towards the bathroom, and once inside, I lean against the closed door, closing my eyes.

The quiet of the bathroom is a shock to my system and all I hear is the pounding of my heart in my ears.

Opening my eyes, I look at my reflection in the mirror across the way and see a wound-up woman in need of a night where she doesn't have to worry about anything besides *feeling* whatever it is Vinny will make her feel. *Make me feel.*

The thought of having more of Vinny's hands on me, all over me, has my heart quickening and my core clenching. I take a deep breath and wait for my heart rate to slow again and my head to clear, which allows me to hear my phone vibrating in my purse.

I pull it out to find five texts from my mom and just as many missed calls. My stomach sinks. Three calls are from her, but two are from Atlantic City General Hospital.

What the hell?

My finger trembles as I tap my mom's name and bring my phone to my ear, clenching it so tight, I hope it doesn't crack.

"Lexi, you haven't answered my calls," my mom says in a rush. "Where have you been?"

"Nonno insisted I go out, so I did. I just saw you called.

What's going on?"

"He's in the hospital."

"What?!" I exclaim, panic seizing me. "What happened?"

"There was a robbery. That's all I know."

"Okay, I'm leaving now. Are you going to meet me there?"

"No, honey, I'm in Miami on a business trip with Charles."

"Fine. I have to go," I say in a rush.

I hang up and push the door open to escape, but slam into it.

Dammit.

I pull the handle instead and make a hasty exit, beelining for Cassie.

CHAPTER 3
Vinny

She knows who I am and her first instinct was to walk away. That's new…

That's new and I fucking love it.

Women always want something from me. My money, my dick, the bragging rights of being with a real-life made man, and sometimes even the chance to be Mrs. Carfano despite none of them knowing what that would truly entail.

And then there's this woman, who practically runs away from me to the sanctuary of the woman's bathroom, not sure if a night with me would be worth it despite this inexplicable *thing* we have going on between us.

That thing makes me want to know her even more.

Rubbing my chin, I take a sip of my whiskey.

I was standing at the balcony up here when I saw her walk down the stairs, and I couldn't take my eyes off her. She was like a ray of fucking sunshine I had to follow, and once I had her in my arms, she burned me in the best possible way. I'll burn until I'm ash if I get the chance to feel her under my hands again.

Looking over at Nico, I can't help but smile and raise my glass an inch in salute before taking another sip. My girl's friend is beautiful and looks like just the right amount of uninhibited self-assuredness and crazy for my brother that will keep him on his toes.

My girl, though, she's beautiful beyond anything I've ever seen. She has long dark brown hair that I want to wrap around my fist and pull to tilt her head back to give myself all the access I want to her lips and neck. Then I want to run my fingers through it while she's lying across my chest after I've fucked her until she *actually* can't tell me her name.

I haven't been to Royals in a few months, and only came because Nico is in town and he needed to blow off some steam. He wanted to go to Dark Horse, the strip club we own here in Atlantic City, where all we'd have to do is crook our finger at who we want and she'd eagerly take us to the back room for a private show. But I wasn't in the mood for easy pussy.

I haven't been in the mood for easy *anything* when it comes to women the past six months or so. Easy gets you whatever you want, but not what you need.

My eyes immediately find their way to my girl when she

emerges from the restroom, but her angelic face is stricken with worry, as if she's seen a ghost.

She walks right to her friend. "Cassie, we need to leave," she says urgently, and her friend's head snaps up, coming out of the bubble she's in with my brother.

"What's wrong?"

"He's in the hospital."

Her eyes widen and she untangles herself from Nico to stand. "Let's go."

"What's going on? What's wrong?" I ask, stepping closer to her. Who's *he*?

"I have to go," she tells me without bothering to look at me. She loops her arm with Cassie's and goes to step away, but I grab her wrist like I did before. Lightly, but still enough pressure to stop her in her tracks. "I have to go," she repeats, this time meeting my eyes that are already waiting for her.

"What happened?" I ask again, taking on a more serious tone, no longer flirting.

"There was a robbery at the deli and my grandfather got hurt. I have to get to the hospital."

"I'll drive you," I say instantly.

"That's not necessary. We'll just call a cab."

"Not a chance. I'm taking you."

"You really don't—"

"I'm coming with you," Nico says, cutting her off and lifting his chin to me. "You take the front, Vin."

"You both really don't have to do anything. I'm not looking for any favors. We can take a cab."

My eyes turn to slits. "It's not a favor. I want to take you and I'll get you there faster."

"Fine," she concedes, sighing.

I lead them out of VIP and through the casino, feeling her eyes on me the entire way. When we make it to our private elevator, I punch in a code, press my finger to a small screen to give my print, and then wait to have my eye scanned. Our security is intense, and sometimes annoying when I have to stop and do all of this, but it's necessary to keep our lifestyle under tight control. Security is our family's number one priority. Especially after what happened to my dad and uncle.

No one says anything on the short ride down to the garage, and I lead us over to one of the blacked-out Range Rovers that will fit us all. I open the back door for my girl and her friend, and she doesn't even look at me. I can tell her mind is elsewhere.

I get us to the hospital in record time and park outside of the ER, hopping out right away to open the rear door. A security guard comes rushing out, ready to tell me I can't park here, but with one look at me and Nico, he clamps his mouth shut.

"I'll be back to move it soon," I clip, walking right past him and straight inside to the ER desk. "We're here for Frank Manzato. I need to know his doctor's name and what room he's in."

"I'm sorry, but are you family?" the receptionist asks.

"Yes. My wife is his granddaughter." Jesus fuck, did I just say that? It came out before I could stop myself. I don't even know her name and I'm calling her my wife. "I need the name of his doctor and his room number. Please," I add at the end as a second thought, forcing a smile which has her blinking, staring at me, and then she starts typing something into her computer.

"He's getting a CT scan right now, so it'll be a little while before he's brought back to his room."

"What room?"

"205."

"Who's his doctor?"

"Dr. Weiss."

"Thank you." I flash her a smile that, without fail, leaves her with a flustered and confused look despite being so brisk with her a moment before. It works every time.

"This way," I say to my girl, leading the way.

I feel her eyes on me again, and the quick clicking of her heels on the linoleum has me slowing my stride so she doesn't have to work so hard to keep up. I can't imagine how hard it is to walk in those sexy fucking heels, but I'm grateful to the feminine gods for blessing her with the ability to do it with ease.

Approaching room 205, I slow further, and step to the side so she's the one to walk inside first, but the room is empty. She walks to the windows and turns around, huffing out a deep breath. "How long do CT scans take?"

"Just have a seat and try to relax," Cassie says to her.

"I'll find out," I tell her, needing something to do and knowing I can get answers from anyone. "Nico, stay here with them."

I manage to track down a nurse that I have no problem

charming into telling me everything I need to know, and I return to tell my girl, "He'll be here in a minute. He's awake and alert."

"He is?" Her eyes fill with tears, and when I give her a nod of assurance, she sucks in a sharp breath and quickly swipes away a few tears that escaped her gorgeous blue eyes and started to roll down her cheeks.

"I promise you he's going to get the best care."

"Thank you, Vinny."

"You're welcome…" I trail off, the corners of my mouth tipping up in a slight grin, waiting for her to finish my statement.

"Alexis. Lexi." She finally gives me her name and my smile is instant.

"Lexi Manzato," I say, more to myself than her, and her name rolls off my tongue like it was waiting for me to say it my entire life.

CHAPTER 4

Lexi

Vinny says my name low and to himself, and my heart rate kicks up. He says my name with this Italian lilt I want to hear murmured in my ear the next time he's pressed up against me like he was on the dance floor.

Wait, next time?

Who said he's going to be pressed up against me again?

I shouldn't, knowing who he is.

I should run in the opposite direction and never should've left the club with him in the first place. The club was a safe bubble. But out here? That's a different story with a different ending.

In the club, we were two people who were inexplicably

attracted to one another and were allowed to get lost in a haze of lust and need. Out here though, I'm just the girl from town who grew up learning to play blackjack and poker before I even kissed a boy. Vinny is the guy who more than likely grew up learning to threaten, kill, and help run a family organization that spans I don't know how far and wide, or into how many various illegal activities.

We're too different.

I need to remind myself of our divide. I'm not for him and he's not for me.

"Thank you," I tell him, swallowing the lump in my throat. "You don't have to stay."

He looks at me, and under these harsh fluorescent lights, I must look different than in the dim flashing lights of the club, but he doesn't look away, and neither do I. Our staring match is broken up though, when he has to step out of the way for my nonno to be wheeled in.

"We'll give you some privacy," Nico says, slapping his brother's shoulder as he passes him.

"Nonno," I gush, squeezing his hand. "I'm glad to see you're okay."

"I'm fine, honey. If I was a younger man, I wouldn't have let them get the upper hand on me."

A rush of air leaves my lungs and I pinch my eyes closed. "We can talk about that later. I'm just going to walk Cassie out."

"To the nice young men out there?" he asks hopefully, and I can't help but smile.

"Yes."

"I'm glad you're okay, Mr. Manzato," Cassie says, smiling down at him. "Lexi was very worried."

"She worries too much." He shakes his head, then winces at the motion.

My grin drops, and I lead Cassie out into the hall. "Thank you for everything, I really appreciate it," I say to Vinny and Nico. "Would you mind giving Cassie a ride home?"

"Lex, I can stay with you."

"No, it's okay. I'm going to stay. You go home, though."

"You sure?"

"Yes," I assure her. "I don't know how long I'll be."

"I'll take her," Nico offers, and I see the slight blush to Cassie's cheeks.

"Call me later when you know more," she insists, and I agree before she walks off down the hall with Nico's hand on her lower back.

"Aren't you going to go with them?" I hesitantly ask Vinny who's still leaning against the wall looking too comfortable in a hospital.

"No, I think Nico wants to be alone with your friend."

"How will you get home?"

"I can have someone bring me a car."

"Right." I nod, folding my arms across my chest. "I should go and check on him."

"Of course." His eyes are unwavering from mine. It feels like he wants to say more, but doesn't, and I slowly turn away and walk back into the room.

Nonno is fiddling with the TV remote and I take it from

him, finding an old movie for background noise.

"What happened?" I ask him gently.

"Did you have fun tonight, Alexis?"

"What? No. I mean, yes, I did. I was having fun until I saw all the missed calls from mom."

"I'll be fine, honey. I saw who you were with. A young Mr. Carfano, yes?"

"You know him?" I sputter out, surprised.

"I've been in this city a long time. I know the Carfanos."

I look at the door and then lower my voice to ask, "You know who they are? What they do? Mom warned me about them when I was younger…"

"Oh, she worries too much," he says, which means I at least come by it honestly, I guess. "That family is the heart of this city and they protect their own. You don't want to cross them," he says quietly, "but they are good boys deep down. They understand family and loyalty. I'll have to send Vincenzo his favorite sandwich as a thank you for looking after you tonight."

"Nonno, he didn't look after me." Is it suddenly hot in here?

"Still, he is a good boy."

You could say that, but I wouldn't exactly call him a boy. More like the sexiest man I've ever laid eyes on, and if given the chance tonight, would've let him do just about anything to and with me.

"Whatever you say, nonno."

He smiles softly. "It is whatever I say."

All my pretenses fade and I take his hand in mine.

"What happened tonight?"

Sighing, he rubs his eyes with his free hand. "They got everything, Alexis."

My heart nearly stops. "What do you mean *everything*?"

"I mean everything. I locked up and was counting the money at the register when two men broke in wearing masks and holding guns. They shattered the damn doors, too. Then they demanded I give them all the money in the register. So, I did. But then they said to take them into my office and empty my safe, too."

"How did they know to ask that? That you had a safe in your office?"

"I don't know, but they knew. And when I refused, one of them pressed the barrel of their gun to my forehead and told me if I didn't open it, he'd leave my brain plastered against the wall for my granddaughter to find."

"What?" I gasp, a chill running down my spine. "How? They know me?" I whisper, squeezing his hand tighter to keep from trembling.

"Yes, and I'm sorry, I had to do it. I had to give them everything."

"Why are you apologizing? Of course you did. Your life is more important than money, nonno. It was the only choice you could've made that I would accept. But they were specific about the safe?"

"Yes, and I hesitated, which is when the other one hit me with his gun. *Stronzo.*"

"Did you recognize them? Their voices?"

"I don't know." He sighs and rubs his forehead.

"Who knows about the safe?"

"Just the employees. They know I keep all the cash in there before I pay the bills."

"But everyone is family." Something in his eyes shifts and I narrow mine. "Everyone but the new kid you hired. He's only been there a few weeks."

"He's a good kid. He just needed a chance."

"Yes, a chance to rob you."

"You don't know that."

"You're too nice sometimes, nonno. And no, I don't know it was him for sure, but I will be passing his name along to the police."

He sighs again and closes his eyes.

"I don't want you to stress about it, though. I'll handle everything. You just focus on resting up and not giving the doctors and nurses here too much trouble. As long as you're okay, everything else is okay."

"I love you, Alexis. You're my favorite granddaughter."

"I'm your only granddaughter."

"That doesn't matter. I could still say you're my least favorite, but you're not. You're my favorite."

"I love you too, nonno." Squeezing his hand, I blink back tears, not wanting to cry. "I'm going to go find a nurse to see if your doctor is coming soon to talk about your tests."

Standing, I turn away from him and take a shaky breath in, hiding from him how what he told me scared me.

It has to be that kid. He knows us. It's not like the deli is a place that looks like they're carrying a lot of cash on hand. Plus, nonno's office is a small hidden room beside the kitchen. Why would someone robbing the place even know to ask about an office in the first place?

Stepping into the hall, I close the door behind me and turn to the left to look for the nurse's station when a voice startles me. "A detective is on his way."

"Oh!" I gasp and turn to face Vinny who's sitting in a chair beside the door. "You're still here…"

"I am."

"I thought you were leaving."

"I never said I was leaving."

"You weren't calling someone to bring you a car?"

"No," he says casually, stretching his legs out in front of him. "I said I *could* have a car brought to me. I didn't say I was making that call."

"Okay…why are you still here?"

"I called a friend in the department and he'll be here soon to take Frank's statement."

"You uh…that's not…" I pause, not sure if I should thank him or tell him I don't want his help.

"Lexi, Frank is a friend to the whole city, and I have friends in the department who will make this case their top priority. Although, it seems you already have a lead that will help things along."

"You were eavesdropping?"

"I wouldn't say that."

"What would you say you were doing?" I don't know why I'm choosing to challenge him, but it's kind of fun to see the spark in his eyes when I do.

"I would say that I heard a conversation through an

open door."

"That's called eavesdropping when it's not meant for you to hear."

"Regardless of that," he says, shrugging one shoulder, "he lost everything. And the guys who did this clearly know the both of you."

"I know that," I grind out. "There are only a few people who know about the safe and knows the way he does business." I walk a few a paces past him and then turn back. "I told him keeping his money there was a bad idea, but he never listened. He doesn't like banks."

"He's old school. I understand."

"Of course you do," I say sarcastically, rolling my eyes. "You probably have a lot of cash on hand since you can't put it all in the bank without having proof of its source." Oh my God, did I just say that? I clamp my lips shut.

"I see you have me figured out."

"There's not much to figure out."

"Let me guess. You've seen a few movies and shows, and now you think you know everything about me." I roll my lips between my teeth and stay quiet. "Exactly," he says.

"Thank you for calling your friend, but I have to go find a nurse to see if the doctor is coming soon to tell me what's going on. I also have to figure out if the deli is okay because he said they shattered the doors to get inside, and aside from your friend coming here to take my grandfather's statement, are the police going to the deli? And whose responsibility is it to board it up or whatever so no one else can get in and steal more stuff or go up to his apartment. I don't know anything." Tears well in my eyes and I turn away from Vinny. Panic rises in me and I don't want him to see me cry when I was just judgmental and mean to him.

"Hey," Vinny says softly behind me, placing his hand on my elbow. "Lexi." He turns me back towards him. "When I made my call, he told me officers were already at the deli collecting any evidence they find. The neighbors called it in when they heard the glass shatter. I also told him to take care of it all when they're done. They'll board it up and place crime scene tape over it. Everything is going to be fine. I also have one of my guys out front watching the place."

"You don't have to do that," I say, but he shakes his head at me to stop.

"My family takes care of this community and their own. Frank is a big part of this town, and has been for a long time, so we're taking care of him." His eyes hold mine captive. "And you," he adds, making my heart sputter in my chest.

Why does him taking care of me sound so damn good? I can tell he knows how to take care of a woman, in every aspect of the term. And his kindness is shocking to me. I'm not used to people helping me, but I'll take it right now because I'm so tired of doing everything myself.

"Now, let's go find the doctor and get you your answers."

"Okay," I say softly, and his hand slides down my arm before falling back to his side. "Does that mean you're going to tell them you're my husband again?"

"You caught that, did you?" He smirks, the playful twinkle returning to his eyes. "I said what I had to say. Do you have a problem with it? Or maybe you liked the way it sounded too much?"

Smiling, I roll my eyes. "You need to relax. I've only just met you. And how do I know it's not you who liked the way it sounded too much?"

"I didn't mind it." He winks, leaving me with my mouth hanging open as he walks up to the nurse's station.

He needs to stop, but I also don't want him to stop.

"I need to know when Dr. Weiss is coming to talk to his granddaughter about Frank Manzato and the results of his CT scan," he says to the nurse behind the desk, flustering her with his charm

"He's doing his rounds now. He'll get to Mr. Manzato's room soon," she says politely, practically batting her eyelashes at him, and I have to hide rolling my eyes.

"I'd love it if you would page him to come here now. You can tell him Vinny Carfano is waiting if that helps," he tells her, and her eyes widen.

"Right, of course." She reaches for the phone and pages Dr. Weiss over the intercom, which is when her eyes slide over to me to give me a once-over – sizing me up. I give her a polite smile in return, not letting her think her opinion has any effect on me. I'm not with Vinny. Technically, right now, he's with me.

The doctor shows up a minute later, looking annoyed that he was called away from his routine rounds. "What is it, Shawna?"

"Mr. Carfano is here about Mr. Manzato," she tells him softly, and Dr. Weiss turns his cool gaze to Vinny.

"What can I do for you, Mr. Carfano?"

"I would like an update on Mr. Manzato.'"

"Let me grab his chart and I'll meet you in his room."

"Good. Thank you." Vinny flashes him a grin that's friendly, but at the same, predatory. He knows he's in charge here, and I'm not going to deny that I like him using his power to help me.

Placing his hand on my elbow, Vinny walks us back to the room, but instead of going inside, I take a seat in one of the chairs in the hall. My feet are killing me. They were numb for a while, but now that the liquor is gone from my system and the frantic panic has subsided, the throbbing of my feet in these heels has pushed its way to the forefront of my mind.

Vinny doesn't take the seat beside me, but rather stands beside the door like a personal bodyguard.

"You're making me nervous," I tell him, looking at my shoes and rolling my ankles to relieve some of the ache. "You're acting like he needs protecting even while in here."

"I'm just standing here to give you space," he says, and I look over at him to find a sexy little smirk gracing his lips that I wish I knew the taste of already. "I don't mean to make you nervous, *dolcezza*."

I want to tell him I don't like that one either, but the way he says it has me hesitating, which makes his smirk grow.

"Ah, I see I've found the right one for you. *Dolcezza* it is. And I'd bet everything I have that you really are sweet. Both your taste" – he winks – "and your heart."

"I'm not so sure about that," I tell him, looking away

and ignoring the part about how I'd taste.

"I am."

I smile and scoff. "You don't know me."

"Exactly. And I can still tell."

I roll my ankles again and look up at him, seeing sincerity in his dark gaze.

"Ms. Manzato?" Dr. Weiss comes just in time.

"Yes." I stand and clear my throat, wincing at the pinching of my toes in these damn heels I wish I could take off. "How's my grandfather?"

"He has a laceration on his head from where he was hit with the gun, but the scans showed no swelling in the brain, internal bleeding, or damage."

A breath leaves my body and I sink back into the chair. "Are you sure? He's going to be okay?"

"Yes." He nods.

"Did you run every test to be sure?" Vinny asks, his voice lowering to an octave that rings with authority. "We're not leaving here until every test has been given and every possible injury has been ruled out."

Dr. Weiss looks at Vinny, his lips pressed into a hard thin line. I can tell he wants to argue, but bites his tongue. "Of course, Mr. Carfano. I'll run a few more just to be even *more* certain."

Vinny's eyes narrow. "Thank you."

I wait for Dr. Weiss to walk away before asking, "People tend to do as you say, don't they?"

"Yes. If they're smart, they do."

"And what happens if they're not smart?" He gives me a

little smirk and leans back against the wall, shoving his hands in his pockets. "Never mind. I shouldn't have asked when I know the answer."

Vinny rubs his thumb across his bottom lip. "You still think you have me figured out."

I don't.

I really don't.

"Vinny." A man approaches us and he and Vinny shake hands.

"John, how are you? Your mom?"

"She's well. She's loving her new nursing home."

"Good." Vinny nods. "I hope she takes everyone in there for their money."

The man grins. "Give her time and she will."

"I have no doubt. This is Lexi Manzato," Vinny directs at me, and the man offers me a humble nod of respect. "Lexi, this is Detective John Carthwright. He's going to take Frank's statement and make sure he finds out who did this."

I stand. "Thank you for coming."

"Of course, Ms. Manzato. Would you like to be present when I take his statement?"

"Yes," I tell him, then look to Vinny. "I'll be right in." I wait for the door to close before I say, "Thank you for everything. And thank you for insisting they run a few more tests."

"You're welcome." He's leaning on the wall right beside me, so close that his voice vibrates into me like a plucked guitar string – waves bouncing around my insides.

My dry throat works around a swallow. "You don't have

to stay any longer, though."

"Are you going to be okay?" he probes, raising his hand to brush a section of my hair over my shoulder. He lingers, twirling the ends around his finger.

I nod, my voice silent. He leans in and his lips brush against my cheek, kissing me softly. I close my eyes as the warmth from his lips spreads through me and pools in my core. A soft and gentle Vinny is just as sexy and turns me on as much as the take-charge, hot and heavy on the dance floor Vinny.

"This isn't the end, *dolcezza*," he whispers against my heated cheek, causing my hand to tighten on the door handle in order to keep from falling forward and losing all sense of balance and self-awareness.

Vinny walks off down the hallway and I watch him go, meeting his gaze one last time as he turns the corner and looks back at me.

No, this isn't the end for us.

It should be, but I want to know everything that gaze has the ability to make me do.

I sit and listen to my nonno recount what happened to Detective Carthwright and it's hard to hear, but I keep my eyes moving around the room, cataloguing everything I see to keep myself from getting emotional.

When he gets to the part about the safe and telling the detective how much cash was inside, Carthwright pauses his writing. "You had $80,000 in cash in your safe?"

"Yes."

"It was the deli's earnings for the month so far as well as his entire life's savings," I tell him, and Carthwright doesn't hide his surprise.

"I don't trust banks," nonno adds.

"Who knew you had that much in there?" Carthwright asks.

"No one knew the exact amount or the code but me. But my employees knew my system and knew I only deposited money into the bank once a month to pay the bills."

"Do you have records to show the amount you had in there?"

"What do you mean?" nonno asks, his brows furrowed.

Oh no.

"Do you have accounting books or anything official to prove you had $80,000 in there?"

"I…" My nonno starts, then stops, thinking it over.

I was never a part of that aspect of the business. He took care of everything. He's a very smart man and was always more than capable of handling the books.

"I have my records for tax purposes."

Detective Carthwright presses his lips into a thin line and writes something down. "What?" I ask, slightly annoyed. "What's that look for?"

"It's just that tax forms don't prove anything in regards to the amount stored inside the safe. And if the cash is found, it can't be proven to be yours. It's also an issue for insurance claims. People could make up any amount when making a claim. What's to stop you from saying you had $80,000 in there when it was only $50,000 for example." I clench my jaw. "I'm not saying you're lying or would lie. I'm just being honest with you when it comes to situations like this. You could prove the month's earnings, but not the savings."

"Then what are we supposed to do? Be out $80,000?"

"You'll have to discuss that with your insurance company after we file our report. Mr. Manzato, is there anyone you can think of that would do this? Any disgruntled employees, past or present?"

Nonno looks to me and I give him an encouraging nod to tell the truth about the new kid.

"I hired a local boy at the beginning of the month. Benjamin Pastorelli. I've known his parents for a long time and they said he's been getting into trouble and hanging with people they don't exactly like. He's been okay so far, but he did see me deposit the cash midday last week when he came to ask me a question about a delivery. All my other employees have been with me for at least a decade."

"Hmm," Carthwright hums, jotting down more in his little notebook. "Sounds like he's our best lead. I'll make sure to have him picked up for questioning. Is there anything else you can recall about the two men? What they said, or did?"

"I think I covered it all," nonno says.

"If you remember anything else, please call." The detective hands the both of us his business card and stands. "I'll let you get some rest now."

"Is it safe to go there when he's discharged?" I ask

Carthwright. "His apartment is above the deli."

"Yes, the investigators should be done in an hour or so and will board the front door up to seal in the scene. But I'm assuming there's a back door for you to use?"

"Yes, there is."

"Then you'll be good."

I shake his hand. "Thank you so much."

"I'll keep you updated."

"Thank you," nonno says, shaking Carthwright's hand as well.

He leaves and a nurse comes in a minute later to take nonno for a few more tests as promised. I can tell he's not happy about being fussed over again, but I don't care. I need the peace of mind.

"Miss?" The nurse smiles, turning her head back before wheeling him away. "There's a bag out here on the chair with your name on it."

"There is?" Confused, I stand and curse under my breath at the pain of my feet now radiating up my legs. I grind my teeth and walk into the hall to see a pink bag with a note resting on top with my name scrawled across it. I turn the piece of paper over and smile when I read it.

You look good in those heels, dolcezza.
But these will feel better. And yes, I made sure they
match that sexy dress of yours.
See you soon, Lexi.
- Vinny

I lift the tissue paper and smile when I see a pair of pink fuzzy slippers. I immediately take a seat and undo my heels, sighing the second my feet touch the soft fur of the slippers.

They do indeed match my dress and I like that he even thought about that as a factor when getting these for me. And the fact that he even thought to buy them for me in the first place has me wishing I didn't tell him to leave. I had to, though. He'd already done way more than any other man would have in his place for a woman he just met in a club hours beforehand.

I wiggle my toes and smile again, hating that I want to see him soon, too.

It wouldn't be smart to see him again, but maybe I'm tired of being careful and smart. Maybe I want to be a little reckless.

CHAPTER 5

Lexi

I haven't slept in almost forty-eight hours and I'm on the verge of passing out, but I have to make sure my nonno is settled before I can close my eyes.

There's barely any light left in the day when we get back to the deli, and as I drive past the front to get to the back lot, I see my nonno's face fall at the makeshift plywood door and police notice taped to it.

"It's going to be okay, nonno. I promise. First thing tomorrow morning, I'm going to call the insurance company so we can get repairs underway. You just focus on resting up so you can get back to work as soon as the work is done," I say optimistically.

"I'm tired," he sighs. "I just want to go inside and lay down."

I've never heard him admit he's tired before, which makes my heart hurt. He sounds defeated.

"I'll sort everything out. Don't worry, it'll all work out. You taught me that."

He gives me a sad smile and pats my knee. "Yes, honey. It'll all be fine."

I park in the lot behind the building and we enter through the back entrance. I'm surprised when he walks right up the back staircase and doesn't even make a move to survey the damage out on the floor first. I'll have to sneak down later to clean up so he doesn't try to do it himself in the morning.

"I'll be fine, Alexis. You can go," he says to me when we're in his apartment.

"I'm not leaving you, nonno. In fact, I wish you would come and stay with me for a few days while I get everything sorted out."

"I'm not leaving my home just because some *stronzo* caught me off-guard."

"I figured," I sigh, already knowing how stubborn he is. "I'm going to stay with you, then."

"No. No, you're not."

"Yes, I am. At least tonight, and I'm not taking no for an answer." I can be stubborn, too.

"Fine," he concedes. "One night, and then you go back to your place."

"Whatever you say." I smile, and he shakes his head.

"Do you want me to get you something to eat? I know the hospital didn't have anything you like."

"No, I'm just going to take a shower and go to bed. I couldn't rest in that place."

"Okay, let me know if you change your mind."

"I will." He closes the bathroom door and I hear the water turn on.

I know everyone has their moments of weakness, but I've never seen his until today. He's been my rock and my strength since my dad died, and now it's my turn to be his.

After nonno gets out of the shower, I take one and change into a pair of yoga pants and an oversized t-shirt I still have in the spare bedroom from when I stayed here after his surgery in September.

Braiding my hair, I feel more like myself again after the longest night and day of my life.

I'm exhausted, but I'm also starving, so I root around in the kitchen and throw together a salad for myself and settle in on the couch to watch some TV.

It doesn't take long before my eyes grow heavy and I can't keep them open anymore.

I'm too lazy to drag myself to bed, so I pull the handmade afghan my nonna made from the back of the couch and cover myself in a little of her love, making me drift right off to sleep with thoughts of a man who did more for me tonight before knowing my name than anyone's done in a long time.

"Alexis, wake up." My nonno gently taps my arm.

"What's going on?" I ask groggily, not even sure if I'm awake yet or not.

"I hear voices downstairs."

I bolt upward, fully awake now, with my eyes looking all around. "What?" I throw the afghan off me and stand. "You stay here and I'll go check it out."

"No, I'm coming too."

"Fine, but I'm going first." I unlock the door, and sure enough, I hear men's voices down below in the deli.

What the hell?

I walk down the stairs slowly, and when I turn the corner, I get a peek at what they're doing. It looks to be workers installing security cameras and new doors.

Again, what the hell?

Seeing as they're not here to rob us for whatever we have left, I walk right up to them. "Excuse me, what are you doing?" I ask, and everyone stops to look at me. "Who are you and why are you here?" They all go back to their work except one who walks over to me. "Are you going to tell me who you are and what it is you think you're doing?"

"We're here to install your new security system and doors, Ms. Manzato."

"How can that be? I haven't even called the insurance company yet. Neither my grandfather or me has ordered this. I can't…" I swallow, my eyes flitting to my nonno for a brief second. "We can't pay you for this."

"Not to worry. It's compliments of Mr. Carfano."

"Is that so?" I scoff.

"Yes."

"Does he not think that I can take care of things myself?"

"I can't comment on that."

"Well, what can you comment on?"

"We're just here to do a job we were given."

"And you were told to break in? Because you broke in here to do all of this." I wave my hands around at the men working. "This place was boarded up and you broke in to help? We just had a break-in. Do you know what it's like waking up to—" I cut myself off and take a deep breath. "You know what? Never mind. Where can I find Mr. Carfano? Where is he"

I can tell he's reluctant to tell me, but I level him with a stare that has him humbly giving me exactly what I want. "He's at The Aces."

"Thank you. Nonno, you stay here and make sure they do what they said they're here to do and nothing more."

"Where are you going?"

"To have a little chat with Vinny." I run upstairs to splash cold water on my face, brush my teeth, and grab my purse and go. I'm angry and I don't know why. He's being nice, or trying to be nice, and I don't want him to be.

I don't know where I'm going to find him, but I park near the main entrance and walk right inside. I look around for a moment, and decide my quickest form of action is to walk right up to a pit boss.

"Excuse me, can you please take me to Vinny Carfano? I need to speak with him."

"I'm sorry, ma'am, I don't know who that is."

I can't help but roll my eyes. "Tell him Lexi Manzato is here to speak with him about the random men he sent to my grandfather's deli this morning."

"One second." He relays my message into the earpiece he's wearing, and a minute later, another man shows up.

"Right this way, Ms. Manzato," he instructs. I look to the pit boss for confirmation and he gives me a nod.

"Thank you."

I'm guided through the casino to a gold door where the man puts in a passcode, presses his fingerprint to the screen, and has his eye scanned before the door opens.

Inside, there's a short hallway with a black door to the left and one at the end of the hall.

My guide knocks on the one to the left and it swings open a few seconds later to reveal Vinny standing there, leaving me speechless. His hair is styled, his suit is tailored perfectly to his body, and that little smirk I want to both slap and kiss away is right there on his perfect lips to greet me.

"That'll be all, Manny, thank you." The guard, or whoever he is, walks back down the way we came. "I didn't think I'd see you so soon, *dolcezza*. It looks like you woke up and ran right over here to see me. Miss me already?" His smirk grows as his eyes roam down my body.

Shit.

I look down and see I'm still in my yoga pants and oversized tee. With no bra. Apparently, I overlooked that key piece of clothing in my rush to get over here.

"Clearly," I say sarcastically. "But you weren't thinking

clearly either when you decided it was a good idea to send men to the deli this morning so that my grandfather would wake me in a panic saying he hears voices downstairs, thinking there was another break-in."

Vinny at least has the decency to look regretful. "I guess I didn't think of that."

"No, you didn't think of that." I push my hair away from my face and push past him into his office.

CHAPTER 6
Vinny

Fuck, she's beautiful when she's mad.

Lexi just stormed right into my office like she's the one who owns this place, not me, and I don't even mind.

I want her in my space.

"It's a good thing I stayed with him last night, otherwise he would have woken up to that alone and thought he needed to play the hero again," she says to me, her eyes spitting fire. "I don't need favors from you. I told you that."

"Not everything's a favor," I tell her, my words harsher than I meant them to be. She said the same thing at the club, and I didn't like it then either. I don't want her in my debt. I want to make her life a little bit easier. "I don't expect anything in return."

"Good, because you're not getting anything in return. I can handle this all on my own."

"You seem to handle a lot on your own."

"Yes, that's what I do. I'm used to it."

"I respect that, but I have just one question." I rub my jaw and her eyes follow my movements. They linger on my lips before she meets my eyes again.

"What?"

"After you asked the men why they were there and who sent them, your first instinct was to drive right over here and demand to see me so you could yell at me?"

"Yes." She tilts her head slightly. "And?"

"I just wanted to confirm that." I give her a little grin and her eyes narrow, suspicious of my train of thought.

"Why?"

"Because I haven't stopped thinking about you, and now I can see how seeing me again makes you feel." My gaze drops to her pebbled nipples poking against the cotton of her dark grey tee and I scrape my teeth over my bottom lip.

I want to know what shade of pink they are.

I want to know what sounds she'll make when I pinch and pull on them.

I want to circle my tongue around them until they're so hard she's hurting, and she cries out for me to relieve the pain.

Lexi crosses her arms over her chest and I shake my head.

"Don't hide from me." I ring my fingers around her

wrists and pull them from her chest, bringing them back down to her sides.

She stormed over here like a little hellcat, ready to sink her claws into me. I would let her, too. I want her scratches down my back while I fuck her senseless and she fights her orgasm.

She gave me a taste of her fight the other night and I want more. She was gorgeous in her sexy little pink dress with her hair and makeup done and heels that made her legs look a mile long. But that was gorgeous like the sun setting and the moon coming out. And right now, she's gorgeous like a sunrise. Soft, innocent, still a little sleepy, but still holding a raging fire ready to set the day on fire.

That big t-shirt has me wanting to find out what she has going on under there just as much as her tight little dress did. And the fact that I can see her nipples through the fabric right now...*fuck me.*

She's beautiful.

I knew she wouldn't accept my help willingly based on how much she fought me on just giving her a ride to the hospital, which is why I knew she'd come here this morning. I knew she'd give me that fight again, and my girl didn't disappoint.

The longer I look into her eyes, the more the fire in them starts to dim, and then she lifts her chin like a defiant queen and her eyes become bright and alight with challenge. A challenge I've been wanting, and a challenge I'm willing to accept.

I want to see Lexi Manzato laid out beneath me as I fuck

her until her fire consumes us both.

"I came here to tell you that I don't need help. I can handle this on my own."

"I know you can," I tell her, not wanting her to think I see her as some damsel in distress. I don't. I see a sure, confident, and strong woman. But I also see a weight weighing heavily on her that I want to alleviate.

"Good." She swallows hard. "I should go," she says softly, her voice sounding anything but sure on that statement. "That's all I came here to say."

"Why is your first instinct to run from me?"

"Shouldn't it be?"

"Yes," I admit.

"Then there's your answer." Lexi's eyes shift away from me and she takes a step backwards towards the door. I follow her movement, matching her steps.

"But is it your answer? You should run, but do you want to?"

She doesn't answer me right away, and instead takes another step backwards, her back hitting the closed door. I step right up to her, leaving three inches of space between us.

I want her to feel this.

Just like when we were dancing, I want her to close the distance. I want her to give in to me so I can give her everything.

"Do you want to run?" I ask again, and her breath hitches. She swallows her answer and I want to feel that swallow around my cock while she's choking on me. "No answer, *dolcezza?*"

At my name for her, her eyes flare and her pupils dilate. She loves when I call her sweetness.

I can tell she has a sweet heart but a dirty mind, and I need both to be mine.

I close our distance by two inches and cup her face. "Are you going to run, *dolcezza*, or are you going to let me kiss those lips of yours I haven't stopped thinking about?"

Her eyes close and her chin lifts. "I'm not running," she whispers, and before she can change her mind, I let gravity bring my lips to hers.

My brain feels like the world spinning on its axis the moment they touch, and I brace myself on the door beside her head to keep from bringing us both to the ground.

Lexi moans into me and I fucking lose all my self-control.

I'm like an animal trying to escape confinement, and I press her up against the door, deepening our kiss.

I lick the seam of her lips and she moans again, letting me inside.

Her hands are on me. She grips the front of my shirt and slides her hands up my chest to grip the collar, trying to bring me even closer. I'm fucking loving how desperate she is to get as close to me as she can.

I cup her tits through her shirt and she moans into my mouth, giving me the sweetest fucking sound I've ever heard. And when I pinch her nipples through the cotton, she tears her lips from mine to give me a throaty moan that's even sweeter.

I press my hips against her when I feel her start to slide

down the door, planting open-mouthed kisses down her exposed throat – loving that she's weak for my touch.

I bite the side of her neck like a fucking animal claiming my prey or claiming my mate. She's fucking both.

One hit and one taste of her sweet lips and she has me delirious.

I want to claim her as mine.

Lexi slides her hands to the back of my neck and moans my name, and I swear it hits me right in my soul, awakening this possessive and jealous part of me I didn't know I had.

I don't want her to moan anyone else's name but mine.

I never want to let this girl go.

My hand drifts under her shirt, and when it touches her bare skin, she sighs, and I groan against her neck.

Her skin is so fucking soft and warm.

I cup one of her perfect tits in my hand. I'm so blinded by this girl and I love the fact that she ran right over here to yell at me without even putting a bra on. I've never been more thankful for a woman to yell at me.

I pinch and roll her nipple, and Lexi chokes on a sob. Dipping my head down, I squeeze her tit and suck her nipple through her t-shirt. She lets out a little scream that turns into a gravely moan that has me wishing I had a recorder. Every sound she makes unlocks another part of me I didn't know existed.

I do the same to her other tit and she repeats that sexy sound for me.

I pull away and look down to see the two wet spots I left on her shirt, and it makes me feel like a king. I slide my hand down to the waistband of her stretchy pants, and just before I can dip inside to find her heaven, she stops me, her breathing becoming erratic.

"Wait. Stop," she pants, breathless, and I pause.

"What is it, *dolcezza*?"

"I didn't come here for this. I can't do this."

I press my forehead to hers and take a deep breath to calm my raging heart and hard-on that's begging for her. "Okay," I tell her, stepping away.

She looks ruffled, like she was just caught doing something bad. I glide my finger along her jaw. "I know you need to run right now, but you probably shouldn't go out there looking like that." I tip my chin down to her chest and her eyes follow, seeing the wet marks I made.

Her eyes widen and she throws her long hair forward to cover my work. "This isn't going to happen again," she says in a rush. "This shouldn't have happened."

"Are you sure about that?"

She looks at me defiantly, that fire back in her eyes. "I'm leaving, and I don't need you to help me anymore. Okay?"

"So, we're back on this," I say, rubbing the nape of my neck.

"Yes, we are."

"Whatever you say, *dolcezza*. But I make no promises. I'm looking forward to you coming back here and kissing me like that again." I wink, licking my lips.

She opens her mouth and then snaps it shut, clenching her jaw. "We'll see," she huffs.

Turning quickly, she throws my door open and storms

out, her hands fisting her hair in front of her to keep it covering her chest.

I can't help but grin as I watch her go and I pull my phone out, dialing Manny. "Escort Ms. Manzato through the casino and to her car to make sure no one bothers her."

"Got it," he says, and hangs up.

I immediately dial Carthwright. "Any leads?" I ask as soon as he answers.

"We went to Pastorelli's home, but he wasn't there, and his parents haven't seen him since that night or know where he went. We're waiting on the fingerprints to come back which won't be right away since we're backlogged. Same with DNA. One of them was an idiot and spit on the floor by the register. It could be the partner."

"Move it all to the top of the pile," I demand. "Whatever it takes, make it happen."

"I'll see what I can do," he mumbles and hangs up.

Yeah, he better do better than just seeing what he can do or he'll be directing traffic by the end of the day.

I wasn't going to get involved aside from fixing the door and installing a security system, but it looks like I need to.

Taking off my suit jacket, I straighten my shirt where Lexi crumpled it in her hands and smile to myself.

She doesn't think she'll come back to me angry again? I'll just have to step my game up and find something bigger to help her with so she'll have no choice.

I decide to call my brother before I determine if I should go to Alec or not with the robbery.

Alec and I run The Aces and we have our hand in

everything that goes on in Atlantic City. This is our territory, and we shut down anyone who tries to have any foothold. We had a challenge with the Triads about a year and a half ago when they tried to start their own underground gambling operation here, but we shut that shit down real fucking quick. They even took Alec's girl as leverage, but that only signed their death sentences in blood. No one fucks with us.

My brother, cousins, and I hadn't had to worry about having someone that meant so much to us that could be used as leverage or a threat before that moment.

Adding someone to our lives is a risk that none of us wanted to take. In fact, I know Alec and his brothers made a pact with each other that they wouldn't let a woman become their weakness. Their dad, Michael, who was the head of the family before Leo took over after his death, was a man who raised his sons to be in his likeness.

He had a ruthlessness that was unmatched and he was tougher on his own kids than he was his nephews. That doesn't mean we don't all have the same Carfano blood running through our veins, though. We know how to turn into ruthless pricks who show no mercy when it comes to protecting what's ours. Both in our business and personal lives.

"Hey, brother," Nico says when he picks up my call. "You come out of your room yet with her?" I can hear the smile in his voice.

"Shouldn't I be asking you that?"

His dark chuckle is all I need to let me know he's been in bed with my girl's friend for at least one night. "Let's just say

I haven't gone back to the city yet."

"Good. I need your help."

He pauses, then says with no trace of joking, "You in your office?"

"Yeah."

"I'll be right down."

I don't ever ask Nico for help, so he knows I'm serious, and fifteen minutes later, he's standing in my office.

"That was fast."

"I left a beautiful and crazy freaky woman in my room to come down here. What do you need?"

"The investigation into the break-in at the deli. I have one of our detectives on it, but one of the guys they think did it is in hiding and they don't know where he is or who his partner is."

"Okay, what does Alec want to do?" I don't answer him and he levels me with a look. "You haven't told him?"

"No."

"I'm going home in the morning. You need to make a plan with Alec, not me."

"I know," I say, rubbing my forehead. "I just thought I could stay out of it. She wants me to stay out of it, and I don't want to explain to anyone why I'm so invested in this yet."

Nico laughs, taking a seat in the leather club chair in front of my desk. "Vin, come on. A beautiful woman needs help only you can offer her and you're trying to stay out of it? I saw how she looked at you in the club. And when she realized you were going to stay to help at the hospital? Vin, she looked relieved. Trust me when I say that women are fully capable of handling their shit, but that doesn't necessarily mean they always *want* to."

"You're an expert at reading women all of a sudden?"

"I've always known what women want, brother." He smirks, the damned bastard.

"Alright, so tell me then, what I should do when a woman who told me she doesn't want my help anymore still kisses me like the world is fucking burning?"

"It depends what you want from her after that?"

I don't even hesitate in my answer. "I want everything."

"Then you need to help her anyway. Let her see your sincerity, Vin."

Nodding, a plan starts forming in my head. One where Lexi won't be able to resist coming back to me even angrier than today. And I can't wait.

CHAPTER 7

Lexi

"Hey, Lex, how's your grandpa doing?" Cassie asks when I call.

"He's better. He thinks he's ready to jump back into working once the doors are installed."

"Lex, I know you're super protective of him, but I think going back to work might just give him some sense of control again after everything."

"I know," I sigh, rubbing my forehead. "The doctors cleared him, too."

"Is the deli going to open soon, though? Did you already get the doors fixed?"

"In a sense," I say.

"And that means?"

"It means this morning my grandfather and I woke up to men working downstairs installing new doors and a security system with cameras and everything."

"How's that possible?"

"Vinny."

"Vinny? Seriously?"

"Yes."

"Oh, big mistake on his part." She chuckles. "What did you do?"

"I went and yelled at him, and then he kissed me."

"AH YES, Lex! How was it?"

"Not the point."

"It is so the point. And if his brother is any indication of what runs in those hot family genes, then you'll be in for a *big* surprise soon."

"Cassie! Did you have sex with Nico after you left the hospital?"

"Yes," she says cheekily. "In fact, I haven't left his room since."

I'm stunned silent for a moment. "You've been with him for almost two days now?"

"Mhmm," she hums happily. "And Lex, oh my God, I don't know how I'm supposed to go back to my mundane life when he goes back to the city. I think I'm in some alternate universe where the world is standing still as long as we're in bed. And the shower. And the couch. And the–"

"Okay, okay, I get it," I say, cutting her off. "Cass, has he told you his last name yet?"

"No. Last names haven't come up. Why?"

"He's a Carfano, Cass."

"Okaaay?" she drags out, not getting it.

"The Carfanos, Cassie. They own The Aces."

"Really? Nico didn't even use that to brag."

"Yeah, what a great guy," I deadpan. "You're clearly not getting it. His family…" I guess there's no way around it. "They're in the mafia," I whisper, not wanting to even say it out loud. "It's dangerous to get close to them."

"I've always liked my men with a side of danger," she says casually.

"Cassie," I berate. Except, I'm not one to talk.

I stopped it, though.

Barely, but I stopped it.

"What? Lex, come on. It's not like anything is going to come of Nico and I. It's just a few days of fun. Mind-blowing fun. But still, just a few days. He's going back to the city and I'm staying here. It's no big deal."

"I just want you to know and be safe."

"And I appreciate that," she says, her voice softening. "I'm safe, Lex. Besides, you know where I am, and if you don't hear from me tomorrow, then you know exactly who to go to for answers."

"That's true." I find myself smiling despite my worry for Cassie's lack of worry. "Alright, I have to go. I have to call the insurance company to get the ball rolling on this claim."

"Will the fact that Vinny already fixed the door and installed a security system be a problem for that?"

"I don't know. I have the pictures from the police as

evidence of everything, along with their report, so I'm hoping it's okay. If not, then Vinny will have more to answer for."

Cassie's throaty laugh fills my ear. "I'm more than certain he wouldn't mind in the least."

And that's exactly what he's hoping for…

"I better go," I tell her. "I want to be able to give my grandfather some good news."

"Alright, call me tomorrow. I plan on enjoying my last night with Nico."

"Yeah, yeah, yeah. Go devour him a few more times."

"You should take your own advice. Bye, Lex!" Cassie hangs up quickly, making sure she gets the last word in.

Shaking my head, I flip through the files in my nonno's office until I find the insurance policy and phone number. He's upstairs cooking, and I really want to be able to take away some of the guilt and burden he's feeling right now.

"Good afternoon, this is Atlantic Coast Insurance, how can I help you?"

"Hi, my name is Alexis Manzato, and I'm calling on behalf of my grandfather, Frank Manzato. We had a break-in a couple nights ago and I wanted to file a claim."

"Do you have your policy number handy?"

"Yes." I read off the number and I hear her clicking away at her keyboard.

"Okay, did you file a police report?"

"I did, but the investigation is still happening."

"Alright, I will need a copy of the report. Can you tell me about what happened?"

I reiterate the story, and when I'm finished, she offers

her sympathies. "I'm so sorry your grandfather had to go through that, and you as well for having to witness the effects of such a heinous act."

"Thank you."

"I'm also sorry to have to tell you that your grandfather's policy doesn't include crime coverage."

"What?" I whisper, my mind reeling with what she's saying. "That's a separate thing?"

"Yes ma'am. He has commercial property insurance, but it's an old policy and hasn't had any updates, add-ons, or adjustments since it was created."

"But–" I say, and then stop, needing to not lose my cool right now. "What does his policy cover?"

"It covers property damage, bodily injury on the job, product liability, libel, slander, copyright, natural disaster, and fire."

"So, there's nothing that can be done about the cash stolen?"

"I'm sorry, ma'am, no. But even if you did have coverage, if it turns out to be someone who was employed at the time, that would void any coverage anyhow."

"It was all he had, and without it, he has nothing. How is he supposed to ever retire?"

"I wish I had better news to give you, Ms. Manzato."

"Me too."

Hanging up, I toss my phone on the small desk and hang my head in my hands, letting the tears that have been building up fall freely.

What am I supposed to do?

My nonno doesn't deserve this. He's worked hard his whole life and deserves to live the rest of it comfortably without worry. He can't work forever.

I only allow myself to cry for a few minutes before I take a deep breath and wipe my eyes. I know what I have to do, and while I don't necessarily like it, it's what has to be done.

CHAPTER 8

Lexi

Shimmying the dress up my hips, I loop my arms through the straps and reach behind me to zip it up. I meet my eyes in the mirror and the girl looking back at me is one I recognize, but also *not*, at the same time.

It's the girl I was for years, slipping into this role for a few hours at a time. I do my hair and makeup, put on a dress and heels, and I play pretend. At least, I think I've been playing pretend. I can't tell anymore.

Sometimes it feels like my everyday life is pretending. But what isn't pretending, is me going to the deli and helping my nonno. Seeing the smiles on people's faces when they walk through the door, and seeing the enjoyment they have in our food and coming together with friends and family over a good meal. Anything can be a celebration when good food is involved.

We bring people together and I love that.

It's a life I would love to wake up and do every day. But my nonno always insisted that I go to college. Neither he nor my nonna had the opportunity to, and when my father chose not to, my nonno insisted that I do. He wants me to have more than he ever did, but I don't think he realizes how much he truly has in life, and how much I want that too. The beautiful simplicity of living and loving and enjoying what you do every day while putting smiles on people's faces is something I want too. It's what I consider a rich and full life.

I chose to fulfil his wishes though, and my dad wasn't around to tell me it was okay if I didn't. I'm going to finish. I only have two semesters left. But I don't know what I would even do with my degree.

I chose psychology because it had a lot of classes I was interested in. I love learning how the brain works, how people work, and how people think, act, and react. But I don't know what I would do with my degree.

I think that's what I've been struggling with and what's been holding me back from thinking about anything in my life past this next year. Taking care of my nonno and finishing school is all I'm concerned with right now. Which is why I've been lying to nonno all week. I told him everything was okay and that the insurance money would come in once the police report was looked over and blah, blah, blah.

He was so happy. There was no way I was going to tell

him his life's savings was gone and he'll have to start all over again. So, here I am, getting ready to go out for the first of many to win back everything that's been lost. Plus a little extra for the improvements I know the deli has been needing.

I'm already lying to him about one thing, why not add that they're giving him more than we expected?

I like to switch up my look every time I do this so I never catch the eye or am remembered by anyone. Which is also why I don't go to the same casino more than once a month. It helps that there's nine of them to choose from. Well, ten if I count The Aces, but I don't, and I plan on staying as far away from there as I can. I don't need to run into Vinny.

Tonight, my persona is going to be the ditzy first-time gambler who gets a little too drunk and goes on a winning streak. I'll be all excited and confused and think it's all just crazy luck.

But it's never luck.

I always win.

CHAPTER 9

Lexi

Opening the safe in my closet, I place the $4,000 I won tonight inside, beside the $7,000 I won the previous two nights.

This was a good weekend, but I'm exhausted.

I spent the mornings helping at the deli, my afternoons reading for next week's classes, and then my nights at a blackjack table.

It's going to take me quite a few weekends to reach $80,000, and even more to make enough for the improvements I want to do.

After a long, hot shower, I put on my comfiest sweatpants and a baggy t-shirt, braid my hair, and crawl right into bed, with sleep finding me instantly.

My alarm comes too quickly at six, and I groan, turning over to bury my face in my pillows. But when it goes off again, I force myself to get up. I want to go to the deli for a few hours before my ten o'clock class.

I go through my morning routine and then throw on a pair of jeans, a white t-shirt, and a beige oversized cable knit cardigan sweater.

I undo my braids, but since I did them wet last night, they didn't dry all the way to form nice waves, so I redo the two Dutch braids. After applying a basic, natural makeup look, I slip my feet into my white sneakers and grab my large shoulder bag I use for school.

I only stayed a couple nights with my nonno after the break-in and then returned to my apartment. He was back to his old self and strength, and we both love our independence too much to have me hovering around like he's about to faint at any moment. On my way over to the deli, I'm singing along to a song on the radio, lost in my own thoughts, which is why it takes me a moment to register that the men working on the sidewalk are right in front of the deli.

They're back again?

What the hell?

Are they doing something to the windows?

Instead of pulling around to the lot in back where I normally park, I pull right into a spot out front on the street.

You've got to be kidding me.

He didn't…

He wouldn't…

Vinny's got some nerve.

I sure as hell didn't schedule this, and I know nonno didn't, so that leaves the man trying to get under my skin.

Throwing my car in park, I hop out and walk right up to the men installing new glass front windows. "What's going on?"

They all turn to look at me, but it's the one who was leaning against the front of his car looking at his phone that straightens and walks up to me. "Ms. Manzato."

"You again," I clip. "What are you all doing here? And I swear to God, if you tell me Vinny sent you, I'm going to strangle him."

He smiles. "I'll let him know you said that."

I cross my arms. "Please do."

"Mr. Carfano thought you needed new windows to go with your new doors and security system."

"Did he? That's a little presumptuous of him. Our windows were just fine."

"If you say so."

"I do." I'm lying, though. They were like fifty years old and drafty as hell, but I'm not about to tell him that.

"They're bullet resistant, too," he tells me.

"Is that supposed to be a selling point? We don't need bullet resistant windows. I don't live in Vinny's world where that must be a necessity of his everyday life."

The guy smirks and is about to say something back, but my nonno walks outside and he chooses not to.

"Alexis, good morning." He smiles, kissing my cheek.

"Morning, nonno."

"You didn't tell me we were having work done today."

"Yes, sorry, there was a last-minute opening with this company and I forgot to tell you. I didn't realize they were going to come so early, though. I was going to tell you when I got in today."

"Oh, alright," he says, watching them work.

"I'll be inside in a second and we can talk about it. I just want to clarify something with them first."

"Sure."

He heads back inside and I turn to the guy. "Tell Vinny I don't need his help and he knows that. I also don't need the trouble of lying to my grandfather, because I sure as hell am not telling him the real reason you're here."

I walk right inside and sit at the table nonno is currently wiping down.

"I know you're lying, Alexis. Talk to me."

"I'm not lying, nonno. I just..." I sigh, folding my fingers in front of me.

"I know we didn't get any insurance money yet, so what's going on? Are you gambling again?"

"You act like you weren't the one who taught me how, and you know it's how I've paid for college."

"I know, but–"

"No buts. You need the money, and you're not going to get anything from the insurance company." I didn't want to tell him, but I've never been good at lying to him. Better yet, I don't *want* to lie to him. "We need the improvements and the insurance money isn't going to come."

"What do you mean?"

"You don't have crime coverage. And since Ben more than likely did it, and he was an employee at the time, that's not covered even if you did."

The look in his eyes says it all. He feels like he failed.

"You've helped me my entire life, nonno. Now it's my turn to help you."

"You shouldn't have to."

"If dad was still here, he'd do anything to help you. But it's me here. So, I'm going to do whatever it takes. You need the money and I have the ability to get it for you. It's as simple as that." I give him my best serious stare and he sighs again.

"I don't like this."

"You don't have to like it. But either way, I'm going to keep winning you money and using it to give my favorite place a little facelift."

"What kind of facelift?" he grumbles, and I smile.

"I was thinking a new sign and awning out front. New floors, tables, chairs, and a fresh coat of paint. No drastic changes. Just a newer version of what everyone knows and loves. Maybe even a couple benches outside so people can sit and enjoy coffee and a pastry."

"Fine," he says after a long moment. "As long as you don't make my place some hip joint where everyone who comes in has their phones out instead of talking to one another."

A short laugh bubbles out of me. "I wouldn't dream of it, nonno."

"Good." He nods. "Fine then. Now, go ask those hard-working gentlemen if they'd like anything to eat or drink while I finish opening up."

"I think they're fine," I say automatically, not wanting to feed the lackeys Vinny sent to do his bidding.

"And I think you were raised to be polite."

"Yes, nonno. Let me start the coffee first."

"Thank you, honey. Do you want your favorite sandwich?"

"Yes, please." He knows I'll do just about anything for a pork roll, egg, and cheese on an everything bagel. Especially when it's a bagel from the bakery that delivers fresh every morning. I love getting one within the first couple hours of delivery.

After I press brew on the large coffee makers, I head outside. "So, I didn't catch your name earlier," I say to the guy leaning against his car supervising the workers.

He grins. "Jimmy."

"Well, Jimmy, when you're done out here, you and the guys can order anything you'd like. Coffee is brewing right now, too."

"Thank you."

"You can thank me by telling Vinny to stop all of this." Not waiting for him to respond, I walk back into the deli and pour myself a strong cup of coffee.

CHAPTER 10
Lexi

Déjà vu.

I'm having déjà vu.

I pull up to the deli on Wednesday, and Jimmy and the crew is back on the sidewalk, this time taking down the awning and the Manzato's Delicatessen sign.

There's a new sign leaning against the exterior to be put up, and I hate that I like it.

I park out front again and walk straight up to Jimmy. "So, he decided not to listen to me?"

"Looks that way." He smirks, the arrogant bastard. "But I have this for you today. From him." Jimmy hands me an envelope and I take it and turn away from him before opening it.

Lexi,

I'm going to keep being an inconvenience until
you come and tell me to stop yourself.
See you soon, *dolcezza*.

- Vinny

The pair on him.

Walking over to my car, I grab a pen from my bag and write my response. Folding the note, I slip it into the envelope and hand it to Jimmy.

"You can give this back to him."

"I'll make sure he gets this when we're done."

"I'd expect nothing less from his errand boy. You can also tell him he's lucky I like the sign. Or, unlucky, actually. Because if it was ugly, I would've gone to yell at him like he wants."

Jimmy just smiles and slips the note back in his pocket while I walk inside for my morning coffee.

CHAPTER 11
Vinny

"How's Tessa?" I ask Alec, taking a seat in his office with my coffee in hand.

He narrows his eyes. "She's fine, why?"

"Just asking." I shrug. "I haven't seen her in a while and I miss her."

"You shouldn't. And she's busy. And tired."

"Tired? From what? Dealing with your cranky ass?"

"No," he growls, rubbing his forehead.

"Is she sick?"

"No," he growls again, the damn animal. He's always been closed off and guarded, but when Tessa came into his life, he changed. Softened for her. Only her, but still, he found a balance in his life with her.

"What's going on? What did you do, knock her up?" I joke, then pause midway of bringing my cup to my mouth when I see the blank look on his face. "Wait, did you really?" He gives me a curt nod and my smile is instant, hurting my cheeks. "Congratulations, cousin. That's fucking great."

"Is it?"

"Yes, it is," I assure him, and then add seriously, "Because with your kid, you'll be a good father. Better than yours and better than mine. You are who you are in spite of him, and that's exactly how you'll be with your kid. Tessa will make sure of it, too."

Alec looks relieved by my faith in him, and I meant what I said. He will be better than our fathers. His was worse than mine, though. Michael Carfano was a sadistic son-of-a-bitch that would hold training sessions in the back house of his Todt Hill compound on Staten Island for his sons and nephews.

To be fair, there was a lot of physical training like sparring, boxing, knife throwing, shooting, and lifting weights that wasn't sadistic. But then there were the other things he considered training. Like learning torture techniques, and being at both the giving and receiving end of said techniques to learn how to survive and not break.

Michael was the head of the family and harder on Leo, Alec, and Luca – his own sons and heir apparents. Especially Leo, who took over for Michael when he and my father were killed six years ago. But that doesn't mean my brother and other cousins got away easy.

We're all scarred in one way or another by what we endured, but we survived.

Carfanos are survivors. So long as we can, we will.

"How far along is she?"

"Eight weeks."

"I'm guessing security here is going to be upped."

"She has two of our guys with her everywhere she goes when she's not with me. I told her I didn't want her going anywhere without me, or out at all–"

I throw my head back and laugh. "Alec, man, you're fucking crazy. That's not going to work and you know it. Besides, you don't want her escaping your penthouse prison and have her out on her own even more vulnerable than with guards, do you?"

"I know," he growls, pushing his chair back and standing quickly. He walks over to his bar cart and pours himself two fingers of whiskey, knocking it back in one swig.

"Jesus, it's 8am, Alec."

"And? I have a lot on my mind. I already go crazy making sure Tessa is safe, now I'm going to have a goddamn baby to keep safe. An innocent baby. A fragile little thing that can be hurt by literally anything in this fucked-up world."

"But you're not going to let anything happen to it, are you? And you know I'll protect the little nugget with my life. We all will. I'll be the best fucking uncle. The favorite." I grin. "As always."

Alec scoffs. "Sure."

"Do you know if it's a boy or girl yet?"

"No, we'll find out in a few months."

"Imagine having a girl? A little Tessa? Man, you'll be screwed." I laugh, and Alec levels me with his best death glare, his fists clenched on top of his desk. "Okay." I hold my hands up in defeat. "I won't torture you anymore."

My phone buzzes in my pocket and I pull it out, seeing a text from Jimmy.

Jimmy: Finishing up at Manzato's. She wanted me to tell you that you should have chosen an ugly sign so that she'd have been mad enough to come to you like you want.

"What the fuck are you smiling at?"

"Just a text from Jimmy."

"He has you smiling like that? Do you have something to tell me?"

"He's doing me a favor and just gave me an update."

"What's the favor?"

"Nothing," I tell him, typing out a reply.

Me: Did she reply to my note?
Jimmy: Yeah, she did. I'm on my way back now.
Me: I'm in Alec's office.

I slip my phone back in my pocket and look up to see Alec leaning back in his chair, looking smug.

"What?"

He shrugs and types something on his keyboard.

"Is there anything new we need to be concerned with?" I change the subject from *not* talking about Lexi to business.

"It hasn't affected our business directly, but this month, there's been a group of assholes running around our city robbing locals. They've hit three businesses already and we need to step in since the police haven't caught them yet. Locals know to trust us, and if we can't protect them, then we'll be the assholes who let our community fall apart."

"Are they the same ones who hit a deli a couple weekends ago?"

"Yeah, they did. How'd you know? I only had one of our guys brief me on it all this morning after a corner store was hit late last night. The same family has owned and operated it since the seventies."

"I know the owner of Manzato's." I scratch my chin and pick up my coffee cup to take a drink before adding, "And his granddaughter."

"And there it is," he says, raising his eyes to the ceiling.

"Fine, Jesus, I met her at Royals when Nico was here. That night, she got a call saying her grandfather was in the hospital after a robbery, and I drove her there."

"You did?"

"Yeah. I couldn't let her walk away before she even told me her name."

"She wouldn't tell you her name?"

"No." I grin. "She also knew who I was when I told her my name and her first instinct was to walk away."

"That's different for you. I was lucky that by the time Tessa found out who I was, she said she couldn't walk away even knowing she probably should."

"Huh, I thought she was smarter than that," I tell him,

and that death look is back, making me laugh. "You need to relax. Maybe you should go back upstairs and try to put a second baby in her."

"Shut the fuck up, Vin."

"Sorry for trying to help you out." I shrug.

There's a knock at the door and I hop up to get it, knowing it's going to be Jimmy. "Thanks, Jimmy." When I sit back down, I eagerly open the envelope.

Her response doesn't let me down, either. Below what I wrote, she added:

You'll have to try a little harder
since I know your game.

She wants me to try harder? She has no idea how crazy I can get when I want something. Or, *someone*, in this case.

"Are you two passing notes like you're in elementary school?"

"Just a little game we're playing. I'm going to win, though."

"You have too much confidence."

I flash him a cocky grin. "No such thing."

The taste of Lexi's lips and the sound of her sweet and dirty moans haven't left my mind since she walked out of my office last week.

Now I need to know how every inch of her tastes and what sounds she'll make when my tongue is licking her pussy and my cock is balls deep inside her, stretching her wide.

Fuck.

Readjusting myself in the chair, I tuck the note safely away in my pocket and clear my throat. "So, I've already got a lead on one of the robbers. His name is Benjamin Pastorelli and he worked at Manzato's for a few weeks before he learned how Frank does business and that he keeps all his money in a safe in his back office. I've got Detective Carthwright on it, but I also passed his name along to our men on the streets to keep an ear to the ground. He clearly hasn't left town with the money he's stolen if he and his partner hit another business last night. He'll surface again."

"You should've told me."

"Probably. But I didn't know they were doing it to more businesses."

"I'll make sure his name goes out to everyone and I'll send a few of our guys to the other businesses that were hit to offer our help and to see if they need anything."

"Good. I don't want anyone thinking I'm playing favorites."

"But you are."

"True." I grin, taking a sip of coffee. "And since we've got all that covered, I'm going to leave you to your morning drink. Unless you want me to stick around to pick out baby names? Because I think Vinny is great for a boy. We'd be lil and big Vin."

Alec rolls his eyes. "You can save that for your own kid."

"Maybe I will."

I leave his office and see Tessa at the end of the hall, walking towards me.

"How's my girl?" I wrap Tessa in a hug. She's been like another little sister to me since she came into Alec's life. Of course, it drives Alec crazy every time I call her that, and he always grumbles, *she's not your fucking girl.*

"I thought I was your favorite?" Her question is mumbled against my chest. I've always greeted her by asking, how's my *favorite* girl?

"Sorry, *sorellina*, but I might have a new favorite."

She pulls back to find me smiling. "What? Who?"

"First, congratulations. I'm going to be an uncle."

"Alec told you?"

"I sort of guessed and then he confirmed it. Was he not supposed to?"

She shrugs. "No, that's fine. We were going to announce it all at once to everyone."

"Announce all what at once? There's more?"

"Kind of." She has this guilty look on her face.

"No," I say. "You didn't. You got married without me?" I pout, and tears gather in her eyes. "Oh, shit. I didn't mean to make you cry. I'm sorry, *sorellina*. It's okay, I promise. I don't know why Alec didn't just tell me, though."

"I don't mean to cry. It's these stupid hormones," she huffs, upset with herself. "We got married a few weeks ago. The day after I found out I was pregnant. We went into the city and Leo and Abri were our witnesses. But you deserve to know before everyone else, too. You've been like a brother to me since we met. And since I lost mine..." she trails off, smiling through fresh watery eyes.

I pull her in for another big hug.

"Thank you for being you, *sorellina*. You're who Alec needs and who this family needs, too. And you know that little girl or boy will be loved and protected. Always."

"I know." She sniffs, hugging me tighter.

"You know, if Alec walks out and sees us like this, I won't be able to win my girl over. Because I'll be maimed. Or dead."

I get my desired response and feel her shake with laughter. "Why do you have to win her over?" she asks, pulling away. "She doesn't like you?"

"She doesn't want to get involved with a man like me. But I've got a plan."

"Well, when she finally gives in, which I know she will because it's hard to resist your charms, I want to meet her."

"You will."

"Good. Now, I've got to go surprise my husband." Tessa winks, walking around me.

Wow. Husband.

Alec is a fucking husband.

I honestly never thought that day would come until Tessa walked, or rather danced, into his life.

None of us wanted to get married. We all saw and experienced the marriages our parents had. All arranged to keep the family line going, and all with someone who understood the life and understood who we are and what we do without judgement and without needing to explain ourselves.

But I've seen my cousins break that mold, and I'd be lying if I said I wasn't envious. I see what's possible and I want it, too.

I love my life, but having a good woman who's loyal and loves you through the good, bad, ugly, and whatever else this life can throw at you, is something we all crave. It's something we all need.

There's always the imminent danger that goes hand-in-hand with the people we do business with, as well as those that want the businesses we have. But protecting the women in our lives and our family is our number one priority.

Over the past year and a half, our family has dealt with kidnappings, fucked-up business partners, even more fucked-up family members, people trying to cheat us, traitors, death, close calls with death, and a whole host of other shit that's just par for the course that is our lives as Carfanos.

I may be crazy for thinking this, but Lexi is my girl. I want her to be the one who breaks the mold and defies normalcy with me.

She's had my attention, my every waking thought, and even some of my dreams, since that first night.

I have this deep-seated need to help her, protect her, and be the one she comes to when she needs anything. But before she can put her trust in me to be that for her, I have to get her to come to me. Which has me needing to put my next part of the plan in motion. It's going to be way past my level of crazy over-stepping because I want to see her again.

Me going to her and trying to convince her to give me any sort of chance isn't the same as her coming to me.

Her coming to me is her entering my space willingly.

It's her choice to look past what she thinks she knows to

hopefully see the man I am.

Taking my phone out, I make a call and arrange what I need for my next step.

Lexi is going to hate it, which means I'll finally see my girl again. And soon.

CHAPTER 12

Lexi

Pulling up to the deli, I smile at the new look. The windows are gleaming and clear, and the new black awning and white wooden sign above it with *Manzato's Delicatessen* written in black script across it makes the whole place look like new.

I can't lie and say I hate it like I want to because they were all ploys from Vinny, and I hate that he's won a little of my good graces because of it. Especially when I saw how much nonno loved it.

I'm sure as hell not telling him it's all courtesy of Vinny, though. I don't want him getting any ideas with whatever Vinny and I are, or aren't. I have too many ideas of my own already.

I keep reliving our kiss in his office with his hands on me, and I keep imagining what it would've been like if I didn't stop him and run away. What it would've felt like to have his hands all over me, with his mouth not far behind.

I've only been with a handful of guys, but none of them were memorable enough to keep me up at night replaying what we did and dreaming of when I'd see them next. And I slept with those guys. I've only kissed Vinny. That just has me knowing sex with Vinny would wreck me, and I've never wanted to be destroyed more than I do by Vinny Carfano.

I drive around the building and park in the rear lot next to my nonno's old pickup.

I walk inside and stop short when I see him sitting at one of the tables with a woman who has a binder out between them. She's quite beautiful, with her light brown hair tied in a low ponytail with a few pieces kept out to frame her face, and very put together in navy dress pants and a white blouse.

"Morning, nonno," I greet, and he looks up with a big grin.

"Morning, Alexis. I've been talking with Lindsay here about updates. Have a seat."

"Hi, Alexis." She stands and shakes my hand. "I'm Lindsay. I'm here to discuss the interior."

"Of?"

"The deli."

"Did you not set this up, Alexis?" Nonno asks, eyeing

me.

"No, I didn't. Did he send you?" I direct at Lindsay.

"Did who send her?" Nonno inquires, looking between Lindsay and I.

"Yes, Mr. Carfano set this up. Is there a problem?" Worry etches her face, not understanding my hesitance.

"Why would Vincenzo send you to talk about updates to my deli?"

Dammit.

"He's trying to get my attention, nonno. That's it."

He studies me for a beat. "Oh, I see. I told you he was a good man, Alexis."

"I don't know about that," I say with controlled anger. "Lindsay, I'm sorry you've wasted your time coming here, but we won't need your services. We'll be handling the interior ourselves."

"Don't be rude, Alexis," nonno chastises.

"I'm not trying to be rude. I just don't need Vinny's help. We'll be paying for, and deciding on things, ourselves. Feel free to tell Mr. Carfano that."

"I will," Lindsay says gracefully, as if she was expecting that to be my answer. She closes her binder and slips it into her leather tote bag. "Have a great rest of your day. Here's my card in case you change your mind."

I take her business card and thank her, knowing I won't be changing my mind.

"Alexis, what's going on?"

"Nothing, nonno. Vinny thinks he can win me over with his money, but it's not going to work."

"Of course not. You're not the type. How about I just send him his favorite sandwich with a note saying thank you, but his assistance isn't needed."

"He doesn't deserve a sandwich."

"Why would he think buying things for my deli would win you over?"

"Because he knows how much I love you and this place, and how devastated I was to see you injured and the deli damaged."

"Is he the one who paid for the other things?" he asks, waving his arm out towards the windows.

"Yes. Against my will."

"Should I be insulted he thinks my business needs everything replaced?"

"No, nonno, that's not it at all. He loves this town and likes to support local businesses and the people who've been here for a long time. He's not trying to insult you. I mentioned in passing how I wanted to help update the deli for you, so now he's using that to make himself look better to me."

"He's trying very hard, Alexis," he points out, giving me a knowing look.

"I know. He won't take no for an answer."

"Why won't you go out with him?"

"Because he's a Carfano, nonno," I say, as if that should explain everything.

"And?"

"And that means he's the last man I should go out with."

"Just because he's a Carfano, doesn't mean he isn't

worth your time. Do you think your nonna thought highly of me when she first met me? A field man working on her family's vineyard?"

"Yes, I do."

"She never looked down on me for being a poor laborer, but she didn't see me for who I am until I put myself in her path. Vinny is just putting himself in your path, and maybe he's meant to be there."

That's the problem.

I've been starting to think that despite all my efforts to avoid him and not think about him, I haven't been able to.

But this is too much now.

He crossed the line sending that woman here. I never told him I wanted to make improvements to the deli, and him taking it upon himself to get us anything other than new doors and a security system is offensive.

I guess he's going to get what he wanted though, because I'm pissed the fuck off. But instead of going to him like I did last Monday, I have another idea in mind.

CHAPTER 13
Lexi

Swiping red lipstick across my lips, I rub them together and run my fingers through my curls to break them up.

I grab the dress I laid out on my bed and slip it over my head, careful not to ruin my hair or makeup. This dress has been sitting in my closet for so long, begging to be worn. I had nowhere and no reason to wear it until now.

It's made of a shiny, silver, metal-like material that hangs and moves like water on my body. Two thin straps hold it up with a plunging neckline and slits on each side that go from the hem at mid-thigh, up the rest of my leg.

It's a dress that's meant to seduce, tease, turn heads, and make an impression. And that's exactly what I want to do.

This game with Vinny ends tonight.

I leave my coat in my car and grab my small clutch that only has my ID and a thousand dollars cash in it.

I never usually start with that much, but tonight is different. Tonight, I'm going to win until they stop me.

I take the elevator to the main level, and as I walk through the lobby to get to the casino floor, I feel the eyes of those I pass lingering, but I keep my eyes ahead of me.

Once I step down into the pit, I follow the black and white marble path laid out between the black carpeting where the machines and tables are.

I keep walking until I find a blackjack table that has four men already seated at it, and I stop, waiting until fresh decks of cards are placed in the dispensers before sitting in the far-left chair.

Reaching into my purse, I pull out my cash and slide it across the table to the pretty dealer. "Change, please," I say to her, and she nods, taking my cash and spreading it out on the table to count.

I smile at the men around the table and one raises an eyebrow at my buy-in amount.

"Sorry, gentlemen. I hope you don't mind me joining your table."

"Of course not, beautiful. If you need help with the rules or how to bet and when to stop, you let me know." He winks.

"I will," I tell him, keeping my smile intact while rolling my eyes internally.

The pit boss verifies my buy-in amount and nods to the cameras above us while the dealer slides my chips across the table to me.

Let the fun begin.

I'm up fifty grand, and the man who so generously offered to help me understand the rules, has since shut up and stuck around to watch me win well after he lost all of his own money.

I've progressively upped my bets with each new deal, and when the waitress delivers my third drink, I notice it's considerably stronger than the previous two. I smirk to myself. I know the bartender was told to feed me a stronger drink in an attempt to throw me off my game.

Little do they know, it won't work. But I like knowing they've taken notice of me.

I sip my drink slowly and tap the table to signal to the dealer to deal me another card.

Nineteen.

I wave my hand over my cards to stay, and since I'm in the last seat, it's the dealer's turn to flip her card, and I smile when I see a nine and an eight. I win.

I keep sipping my drink slowly, and I keep winning. Counting cards is a skill I developed over years of playing and practicing all through my teen years when my nonno would let me join in on his weekly game nights with his friends. I learned blackjack and poker from them, and the older men always encouraged me to use my brain when playing.

I learned their tells and perfected my own poker face.

They were like extra grandfathers to me, and one-by-one, they've all left. Whether it be into nursing homes or assisted living facilities, or they've passed on, the men that helped me become who I am are with me every time I use what I learned with them. I'd like to think they'd approve of my little revenge plan right now.

When my glass is empty, another appears, just as strong as the last. This one, I only stir and take baby sips from to appease those watching me.

I'm not going to lie, this is fun.

I've always put a limit on myself and made sure I wasn't noticed. But wanting to be caught is thrilling.

My chips keep stacking up and stacking up, and eventually, the pit boss comes up to me.

"It looks like you're having a good night, Miss."

I smile up at him. "I'd say a great night."

"Yes, and I think it's best you call it a night. I'm going to escort you over to the cashier's window so you can cash out."

"Oh, I didn't realize I was finished playing," I say innocently.

"You are." His face remains stone cold.

Turning in my chair, I cross my legs and sip my drink. "Are you kicking me out" – I look at his nametag – "Gerardo?"

"I'm strongly suggesting you're done for the night."

"That sounds like a polite way of kicking me out."

"It is."

"What if I refuse?"

"Why would you? I'm letting you cash out and leave. That could easily change."

"Then let's go cash out."

Standing, I place my chips in the trays the dealer hands me and stack them.

"I can carry those for you, Miss."

"I'll let you carry half." I wink. "They're heavy."

As we're walking over to the cashier's window, Gerardo stops and presses his finger to his ear.

"Repeat that," he says, his brows coming together. "Got it. We'll wait where we are."

"Let me guess, Mr. Carfano has someone coming to get me?"

His eyes study me, a million questions in them that he wouldn't dare ask. "Yes. We'll wait here."

"What about my winnings?"

"I've been instructed to cash them out for you and deliver them when I'm finished."

"Can I trust you to do that?" I ask, knowing I'm just being a smartass for the fun of it.

"Yes, Miss. I'm under strict orders."

"Of course you are." I smirk, seeing another man dressed in all black approach us.

"Miss Manzato?"

"Yes?"

"Come with me."

"Alright." I pass the rest of my trays of chips to Gerardo. "I know how much is here. So don't think I won't count my money when I get it."

"Of course, Miss."

Oh, how the tables have turned.

I follow the guy sent to escort me wherever Vinny has told him to take me, not bothering to ask where that is.

I can't wait to hear what Vinny has to say about me taking his casino's money. I have no doubt he didn't expect this from me.

CHAPTER 14
Vinny

I just checked in with the backroom, and we have a full room tonight. When my father opened The Aces, he created a hidden back hallway and room that's strictly high stakes, no holds barred gambling.

The only way to access it is by invite or referral, and we offer a place to win without having the government take half your earnings. We take 25% instead.

We have signal jammers in the room to protect both us and our players, so it's not until I step out of the hidden door that leads me back to another hallway off the main floor that Javie stops me.

"Hey, boss, there's a girl at one of our blackjack tables

that's been flagged. She's been playing for a couple hours now and keeps winning."

"How much is she up?"

"100 grand. Give or take. She's being escorted to the cashier's window now." He hands me the tablet in his hands that has a live security feed of one of my pit bosses escorting a woman in a sexy little silver dress through the casino.

Tapping the screen, I switch to another camera angle and smile like a goddamn madman.

"What is it, boss?" Javie asks, confused by my smile.

"I want you to go and get Ms. Manzato and bring her to one of our holding rooms. Tell Gerardo over your comm to wait where he is for you and then to cash her chips and bring them to me in my office."

"Got it." He nods, not questioning me.

My girl is good at blackjack. I fucking love that. And I know exactly why she came here tonight, and it makes me fucking hard.

I've been walking around in a shit mood all day since Lindsay called and told me Lexi sent her away and to tell me her services weren't needed.

I expected her to storm over here straight away like she did last time, and when she didn't, I thought I went too far.

Yet here she is, taking her revenge by taking my money.

Our holding rooms for cheaters are on the opposite side of the casino, and I'm going to let her get a little comfortable in one before I go to her.

In my office bathroom, I wash my hands, splash water on my face, and run my damp hands through my hair. Patting my face dry, I spray myself with my cologne. If my girl is going to be mad at me, I'm going to look and smell my best. I need all the leverage I've got.

There's a knock at my office door, and when I open it, Gerardo is standing there with a metal briefcase in hand.

"102 grand," he says, handing me the case.

"Thank you. You can go back to the floor."

Nodding, he backs away and I close the door, taking the briefcase to my desk. I pop the clasps and open it, smiling at the sight of the neatly stacked bundles of cash.

Lexi Manzato keeps surprising me, and I fucking love it.

I check my watch and pour myself a finger of whiskey, knocking it back in a single shot. If I was a crueler man, I would let her sit a while longer to make it seem like she's in trouble. But the truth is, I need to see her. I've needed to see her for over a week now.

Closing the briefcase again, I make my way across the casino to the holding rooms.

"Thanks for staying with her. You can go," I tell Javie, who's standing guard outside the room.

"Sure, boss."

I wait for him to leave before I open the door with a smirk already in place. "Well, hello, *dolcezza*. I wasn't expecting to see you again under these circumstances."

"I didn't want you to think of me as predictable."

"I wouldn't dare." I flash her a grin and place the briefcase on the table in front of her. "You're full of surprises."

Lexi turns towards me in her chair and crosses one of

her long legs over the other, both of them on display in that sexy little dress of hers.

She's a sparkling beacon of hope, reeling me into her gravitational orbit until I'm hers, and I want to be hers more than anything.

"Do you mind if I count my money? I don't want to be cheated out of what I earned."

"You don't want *me* to cheat *you*? That's interesting, since you're the one who cheated me and my casino to get this money."

A slow smile spreads across her beautiful face. "I didn't cheat. I'm just very lucky."

"Then I guess I'm lucky, too. You could've chosen any casino in town to cheat in, and you chose mine. But then again, you may have luck on your side as well. Other casinos might not be as nice as I am. They might've just kicked you out without your money and banned you for life."

"Is this you being nice? A hand delivery of my money *and* you're letting me keep what I've earned?"

"Mhmm," I hum.

Half-sitting on the table, I rub my jaw and lick my lips – Lexi's eyes following my every move.

"And how do you know yours is the only casino I've been lucky at?"

My eyebrows raise. "Am I not?"

"I've been lucky a lot over the years. Within reason, of course. But I can say I've never let myself get noticed before."

My girl likes to run her game around town.

Fuck, that's sexy.

"So, you don't normally wear sexy little dresses and run up over a hundred grand in winnings?"

"No." She winks, popping the clasps open on the briefcase. "You're the only one to make me mad enough to do that."

Pulling out a bundle of cash, Lexi fans the edges of the bills and gives me a sly little grin that has my cock hard in an instant. She holds a few stacks in each hand, a proud look in her eyes. "Well, tonight was fun, but I'm going to go."

"You can go when I say you can go," I tell her, and her eyes harden. "This is my casino, remember? I'm prepared to hold you here all night."

"Why?"

"Because I'll take any and every opportunity to spend time with you."

"Even when it involves you holding me against my will?"

"That's the fun part." I wink, and her eyes melt, clearly turned on by the notion of being held hostage by me.

God, she's fucking perfect.

Lexi blinks and her eyes focus on me again. "I came here to prove a point," she says, her eyes now two blue flames. "I don't need your money and I don't need you to fix anything else in the deli. You wanted my attention and you wanted to piss me off enough to come to you, and you've accomplished both. But you've also insulted my grandfather, and I was forced to lie to him when I never have before."

"Why did you have to lie to him?"

"I told him that I mentioned all the improvements I

wanted to do to the deli to you in passing to cover the fact that based on your need to rile me up, he believed you were insulting him and calling his life's work and livelihood a piece of shit that needed an overhaul."

"Fuck," I mutter. "That's not what I intended at all."

"I know. That's why I lied to him."

"I'm sorry you had to do that," I tell her sincerely.

"Thank you."

"Is there anything I can do to make it up to you?" Straightening, I stand in front of her and tilt her chin up with my finger.

"Maybe," she whispers, swallowing hard.

"I was thinking…" I trail off, leaning closer. "I'd start with this."

Lexi's gravity pulls me in and I press my lips to hers.

It takes everything in me to hold back and not kiss her until she's a panting, pleading, and needy mess straight away.

It isn't until she grabs the opening of my shirt to pull me closer that I give her more. And knowing she wants more, and it's not just me, turns me on more than if I just took from her what I know we both want.

Pinching her chin, I slide my other hand into her hair and fuse my lips to hers in a kiss that has my heart racing like a fucking thoroughbred at the derby.

Every rapid beat echoes one word into every cavernous part of my body and soul.

Mine.

Pulling her up by the chin until she's standing, I lift her up onto the metal table, and her dress clinks against the surface.

I step between her legs and pull her towards me until her core is nestled against my cock that's straining to be free.

Everything in me is screaming to fuck her right here and now, but now's not the time or place. I need to convince her to give me a chance. A chance for her to realize what she's feeling isn't a bad thing and isn't something she needs to fight at every turn.

I'm going to push her to the edge and then stop short so she'll be begging me to take that last step and fling us into the unknown. I have a feeling what's over the edge is just as much a mystery to her as it is to me, and I'd greet the dark abyss with a smile.

Lexi moans into my mouth and I bite her bottom lip, making her moan even louder.

I slash my tongue over where I bit her to soothe the flash of pain, and her body melts in my hands.

Lexi scratches at the back of my head and I groan, entangling my tongue with hers. She's a fucking drug, and the only one I have no problem overdosing on.

I wrap her hair around my fist and pull her head back, tearing her lips away from mine and biting her chin.

Lexi cries out and then moans when I kiss my way down her throat.

"Vinny," she sighs, and my cock jumps at the rough and desperate tone of my name coming from her sweet lips.

"Yes, *dolcezza?*" I ask against her skin. Swiping my tongue back up her neck to her ear, I suck on her lobe and swirl my tongue around her stud earring. "Tell me what you want."

She gasps. "I want…"

Lexi's head falls to the side in a silent beg for more as she rubs her sweet pussy against me, trying to get herself off.

"You want my cock, *dolcezza*?" I rasp in her ear, and a moan gets stuck her throat. "Was that a yes?"

She rakes her nails across my shoulders, and I can't wait to feel her do that against my bare skin. I want her to mark her territory like a goddamn animal.

"Yes."

"Hmm," I hum, tugging on her lobe with my teeth. "I don't know if you're ready for it yet."

"Please," she begs, and I chuckle, pulling on her hair again.

"Maybe I should see if you are for myself."

Sliding my hands down her body to her hips, I almost lose it when I touch the soft skin of her thighs. I allow myself only a moment to savor how good she feels before I slide my hands up under her dress.

I grip her bare hip with one and glide my knuckle over her silk covered core, the damp fabric clinging to her pussy.

Fuck.

Lexi moans, and I press my knuckle to her clit. She gasps, her legs tightening around me.

"You're soaked through, *dolcezza*."

"Yes," she sighs, digging her fingers into my shoulders.

"But I think before I see just how wet you are for myself, I should tell you I've changed my mind about letting you walk out of here with that case of money."

Her body stiffens, so I press against her clit again and she shudders, becoming pliant once again.

"Why?" she asks, her voice strained.

"Because that would be too easy." I kiss her below her ear. "But there's a way to get it."

"How?"

I pull her silk thong to the side and glide my knuckle down the bare slit of her pussy.

Fuck. Me.

She's shaven.

Bare. Smooth. Slick.

I lose my train of thought and bite down on the side of her neck before I forget my plan and give her everything she wants without the assurance I'll see her again.

"I'll give you your money. But only in the form of accepting the services of Lindsay."

"What?"

I pinch her chin to get her to look at me. "You can have your money in the form of Lindsay's services. That's a $102,000 budget."

"And if I don't use the whole amount?"

I flash her a quick grin and make another pass of my knuckle through her slick center.

It's getting harder to focus on what I'm saying when my mind is busy picturing my cock sliding into her soft and smooth pussy, enveloping me in a tight, wet, hot hug to welcome me home.

"Then you let me spend the rest on you."

"I don't want you to buy me anything."

"It would be you buying it for yourself. Your money. I'm just the keeper of it."

"Why?"

"Because I want to make sure I get to keep seeing you. Because maybe you'll eventually see I'm not so bad."

"Well, I hate you right now," she says through a clenched jaw, her eyes blazing blue flames again.

"Do you?" I slip my middle finger inside her and she cries out, her inner muscles clamping around me, squeezing me tight.

Fuck, I can't wait to feel her do that when it's my cock filling her and not just my finger.

"If this is you hating me, then I can't wait to find out what you liking me is like." Lexi grunts and I smile, curling my finger inside her to stroke her inner wall. "You can hate me all you'd like, *dolcezza*, but do you agree to my terms?"

"No," she says, and I frown.

"That's too bad." I kiss the corner of her mouth and pull my finger out of her.

"What are you doing?" she asks quickly, gripping my shirt.

"Not playing fair." I wink. "You want me to keep going?"

"Yes," she hisses.

"Then you'll have to agree to my terms."

"That's blackmail."

Laughing, I squeeze her hip and bring my finger that was just inside her to my lips, licking it clean.

Her eyes lose focus and she bites her lip.

"Mmm," I hum. "You are sweet, *dolcezza*. I just wish I could've had the chance to taste your sweet pussy firsthand." I swipe the finger I just licked across her lips and press it inside her mouth.

She swirls her tongue around my finger and sucks it completely inside her hot mouth.

Fuck. Me.

Lexi Manzato is trying to kill me.

"If you're good and agree to my terms, then I'll let you suck my cock and put that tongue of yours to better use instead of wasting it on my finger."

"Are you saying sucking your cock is a privilege I have to earn?" I nod. "So, if I went to my knees right now, you would stop me?"

"I would." She raises her eyebrows in disbelief. "Because it's not about me right now. Sucking my cock won't get you your money."

"But letting you finger fuck me or lick my pussy will?"

"That's right." I smirk, loving her dirty mouth. "You let me pleasure you and you'll get your money."

"But only in the form of improvements to the deli and buying me gifts?"

"Yes. Although, it doesn't have to be your typical gift. If you want to go on vacation or get a new car, that'd work too. Of course, if you want gifts of my choosing, I'd love to see you in lace, silk, and pearls. Actually, just the pearls." I wink.

"I bet you would," she challenges.

"You could always walk out of here with nothing." I trail my finger across her cheek, down her neck, the center of her chest, and over her torso before sneaking it back under her dress and running it up and down her silk covered center. She doesn't get my touch again until she agrees.

I kiss the corner of her pressed lips and pull my hand away again. "Is that what you want? Nothing?"

My stomach sinks when she drops her hands from my shoulders to her sides. For a moment, I think she really is going to walk away, but then she reaches out and circles my wrist with her delicate fingers and brings my hand back to cover her pussy.

"I agree to your bullshit terms."

"You won't regret it, *dolcezza*," I whisper in her ear. "I'm going to make you come harder than you have in a long time." I lick the shell of her ear. "Scratch that. I'm going to make you come harder than you *ever* have before."

I bite her neck and pull her thong to the side, plunging two fingers inside of her.

She cries out, her hand around my wrist tightening with her other bunching my shirt at my hip to keep from falling back on the table.

I kiss my way across her jaw to her lips and whisper against them as I work my fingers inside her. "I've never felt a smoother, wetter, tighter, or hotter pussy in my life, *dolcezza*."

Lexi moans at my words and I kiss her hard.

"Lay back. Let me show you why you made the right choice."

I push the briefcase farther back on the table to make room for her, and she lays back, giving me all the access to her that I want.

I take the sides of her thong in my fists and pull them down her long legs and past her strappy silver heels.

I stuff the damp silk in my pocket and smile down at her when I see the question in her eyes.

"My souvenir for later." I wink. "I'll be using them when I fuck my hand and dream of being inside you."

Lexi's eyes widen and then melt when I run my hands up the front of her shins and push her knees to her sides, pressing them to the table.

"So beautiful," I murmur, seeing her pretty pink pussy glisten under the light above us.

I grip her luscious ass in my hands and lift her off the table, my thumbs reaching between her to spread her lips.

"These rooms are soundproof. Feel free to scream." With a cocky grin, I lean forward and inhale her sweet and musky scent that has my head spinning.

Lexi wiggles her hips, trying to get closer to me, but I tighten my grip on her ass to keep her still.

I look up at her. Her gaze is hot and wild, and I wish I could take a picture of her like this so I can look at it later when I'm beating myself off.

Taking another deep breath, I run my nose up her pussy from her entrance to her clit, coating my nose in her juices so every inhale I take for the rest of the night will be of her scent.

"And when you scream," I add, "I want to hear you scream my name. My whole name. Got it?" I spread her pussy open even more and she bites her lip, holding her sexy sounds in when I want to hear them. "Got it?" I ask again, and she nods frantically. "What name are you going to scream out?"

"Yours," she says forcefully, her anger at me making her wait coming through.

"Yes, but what name is that?" I never knew I liked making a woman wait until now.

"Vincenzo!" Lexi growls, and my face splits into a wide grin.

"That's right, Alexis. I want to hear you scream that out when you're coming on my tongue and around my fingers."

Diving right in like a starved man, I plunge my tongue inside her tight hole and her back arches off the table – a strangled cry coming from her lips and echoing around the small room.

Her inner muscles clench around my tongue and I groan into her, sucking my tongue back out and swallowing her sweet nectar.

She's fucking delicious.

I get a sugar rush to my blood that has me flying high and wanting more.

I lick up to her clit and swirl my tongue around her tight bud – eliciting a throaty moan that has my already hard as steel cock, even more so.

It's fucking torturous, but I would pass up relieving my pain every time if it meant I was eating her pussy instead.

I continue to flick her clit with my tongue and plunge two fingers inside of her. I swirl them in a circle and then spread them apart.

Lexi mutters a stream of incoherent words and my chest tightens, loving that I'm making her come undone. And while I could eat her all night long and still be fucking hungry for more, I want to hear her scream my name even more.

"Vinny, Vinny, Vinny," she chants, her sexy mewls, moans, and sighs of pleasure filling my ears.

Her inner muscles start to flutter and I still my fingers, lifting my mouth to look up at her.

"Why'd you stop?" she asks in a panic, her eyes wild and desperate. It's a beautiful look on her.

I lick my lips. "I have one more thing I need you to agree to before I let you come."

"What the fuck is it?" she growls.

Ah, there's my angry girl.

"Go on a date with me."

Lexi tries to lift her hips, but I shove my fingers even deeper inside her to hold her down.

"Ohmygod," she moans in a mumbled string of words.

"Agree to go out with me and I'll let you come."

"I hate you," she grits out, making me chuckle.

"No, you don't." I wink. "Yes, or no?"

"Yes!" she exclaims, and I smile.

"Alright, then. Let me hear you scream, baby."

"Not your baby. And how about you do something to *make* me scream."

"Challenge accepted."

Curling my two fingers inside her, I suck and bite on her pussy lips until her medley of moans grows louder and louder once again.

I shove my fingers knuckle deep inside her and flick her clit. Lexi shudders, and I know she's ready for the finale.

Pulling my fingers out, she cries out in protest. But that angered cry turns into a scream of pleasure when I plug her with my tongue and circle it around.

I grip her ass and press her to my face so I'm suffocating in her sweet heaven while sucking at her entrance until she's clawing at the table and her legs are shaking.

"Vinny, please," she begs. "Please."

Flattening my tongue, I swipe it up to her clit and suck it between my lips at the same time I plunge three fingers back inside her.

Lexi tenses and then detonates.

"Vin—" she gasps, cutting herself off.

I grunt and shake my head against her pussy to tell her that's not what I want to hear, and I push her further. I press my thumb to her tight back entrance and she bellows my name just how I wanted.

"Vincenzo!" It's raw and real and has my fucking heart racing and my cock leaking in my pants.

Her pussy squeezes my fingers like a goddamn vice, flooding my hand with her sweet nectar.

She's a fucking goddess.

"*Bella, bella, bella,*" I chant against the warm, flushed skin of her inner thigh.

I make one more pass of my tongue through her core and she shudders – moaning.

Pulling her silk thong from my pocket, I use it to clean her up and then put it right back in my pocket for later.

Straightening, I look down at her sprawled out on the table and her heavy eyes look back up at me with unfiltered wonder in them.

I lick my lips. "Thank you, *dolcezza.*" Lexi bobs her head in a lazy nod, and I smile. "Do you want to know why?"

She shakes her head and I step around the table. Tracing her jaw, I lean down and kiss the corner of her mouth and then whisper in her ear, "Thank you for giving me the pleasure of pleasing you." She shivers. "I can't wait to do it again. Maybe on our date tomorrow night."

Lexi gasps and tugs at the hem of her dress, pushing me away to sit up. "I only agreed to that because you weren't going to let me come otherwise."

"Ah, ah, ah." I shake my head. "It still counts. No takebacks. Now, if you're not too spent" – I wink – "I'll walk you to your car. I can always carry you, though. I'd love the chance to get you over my shoulder."

Lexi's eyes narrow. "You'd carry me over your shoulder through the casino for everyone to see?"

"Of course not. There's a back way out of here that leads to the garage."

"Of course there is," she grumbles. "I can walk."

"Hmm, I guess I didn't do my job, then."

Lexi slides down from the table and wobbles on weak legs, reaching back to brace herself on the table.

"I take that back," I say close to her ear, twirling her long hair around my finger. "Just think… If you're losing your balance now, I wonder how you'll be after I fuck you."

I kiss her neck and she gasps, pushing off the table to get

away from me.

Smiling, I open the door for her and we walk in silence through the back halls that lead to the parking garage.

It comes in handy when you've worked a guy over for cheating and you don't want a casino full of people to see him busted up and kicked out.

When we reach her car, I open the driver's door for her and brace myself on the frame when she's seated. "I'll pick you up at your apartment tomorrow at six. Dress warm."

Before she can argue or protest, I close her door and walk back the way I came, grabbing the briefcase I left behind in the holding room on the way to my office.

I pour myself a hefty glass of whiskey and take a large gulp, typing out a quick text to Lindsay to tell her to return to the deli in the morning, and then toss my phone on my desk.

Lexi's sweet scent still lingers in my nose and I pull her thong from my pocket, bringing it to my face to breath her in.

I told her I was going to use them to fuck myself tonight, but I know it won't do. I won't be satisfied until I fuck her or she fucks me with that sassy mouth of hers.

I need *her*.

Which means a cold shower is all I have to look forward to tonight.

CHAPTER 15

Lexi

Damn Vinny.

Damn him and his sexy, talented mouth that had me an incoherent mess that gave him everything he wanted. I was too far gone to know any better.

I'm not used to being so out of control, and it scares me.

He says all the right things and it scares me that I believe him when he does. At least, I *want* to believe him.

Just like I *want* to see him again.

I want something for myself.

I want to feel something other than worry. For my nonno, the deli, my future, school. Everything.

It's a sickness that has seeped into every aspect of my

life the past few months, and I feel like all I do is worry.

The only moments of pure escape have come when I'm with Vinny, which is why I'm willingly getting ready for our date tonight.

He said to dress warm, so I don't exactly know what that means we're doing, but I'm assuming it isn't a fancy dinner or a show.

If I was spiteful, I would dress in my favorite sweatsuit, but I like the way he looks at me too much to do that. Although, he looked at me like I was his favorite dessert he couldn't wait to devour when I was in an oversized t-shirt and yoga pants, so I think I could get away with sweats. But after last night, I'm feeling less spiteful and more…compliant.

I'm sure it's just because I'm still riding my post orgasmic haze. I didn't even mind seeing Lindsay at the deli this morning. In fact, I loved her suggestions, and had no problem spending whatever I wanted since it was money I already earned.

We chose the paint color for the walls, the new flooring, and the new tables and chairs. I even decided to splurge and had Lindsay order booth seating that will line the far wall to create a comfortable, old-school vibe.

Nonno was surprisingly agreeable to everything.

He told me he'd be fine with whatever I chose and that he trusted me, but I still made sure I saw genuine excitement in my choices before I gave Lindsay the final okay to order everything.

When I asked her how much the total was estimated at, I

decided to inquire about updating the small half bathroom we have for the patrons. She said it would be no problem at all and that she'll make sure it matches the new interior seamlessly.

Work is going to start on Monday already with prep work and removal. I know nonno is going to go a little stir crazy not having anything to do for almost a week, but it'll be good for him.

Going through my closet, I pull out my faux leather leggings that are comfortable, but also warm since they don't exactly breathe.

I tried to be casual about asking Lindsay how she knew Vinny, but she gave me a knowing smile and told me she worked with him and his cousin, Alec, on redesigns of The Aces' suites a few years ago.

"Don't worry," she said. "I don't mix business and pleasure. It's bad for business, and Vinny believes the same."

I was glad to hear they didn't know each other because they used to date. I know it's a little petty, but I really wouldn't want to be faced with a woman from his past right now. I can already guess it consists of a long string of beautiful women I would inevitably insecurely compare myself to.

Ugh, I grunt, pulling an oversized cream knit sweater from its hanger and tossing it on my bed.

I shouldn't care about who he's seen in his past, but I can't help it.

Because you want to be different, my subconscious tells me. *You want to be a part of his now and his future.*

My subconscious can be a real bitch sometimes. But also correct.

I know it's a bad idea to want him, and an even worse idea to get involved with him, but that train has already come and passed us by, I think.

I finish getting ready and look at the clock. 5:45. Great, I still have fifteen minutes to kill.

I walk around my apartment and clean what's already clean, needing to keep busy. Except I start sweating instead, and decide a pre-date drink is in order.

I pull an open sauvignon blanc from the fridge and forgo a glass, choosing to chug what's left straight from the bottle.

There's a knock at my door a few minutes later, and my heart lurches, knowing the man responsible for turning my life into a crazy mess these past couple weeks is just on the other side.

I put the empty bottle in my recycling bin and take a deep breath before I open the door to a smiling Vinny.

"Good evening, beautiful." He holds out a bouquet of pink roses for me.

"Thank you. They're beautiful." I hold the door open for him and he closes it behind him while I go in search of a vase.

"I had to get them when I saw them. They're the color of your dress from the club. It's a good color on you."

"It was Cassie's dress."

"Doesn't make it any less of a good color on you."

I look over my shoulder at him, giving him a small smile. "Thank you."

"You're being nice to me," he says, leaning against the counter beside me as I fill a vase with water. "Did I push your nice button last night?" I side-eye him and he laughs. "There she is. I knew your sass wasn't too far beneath the surface."

I put my hand on my hip and glower up at him. "Do you want me to be mean to you? Is that your thing?"

"I like when you're a little mean," he says, reaching out to run his fingertips along the neckline of my sweater that's slipped off my right shoulder. "But I don't want you to always be pissed at me. So, tonight, will you be nice to me, Lexi Manzato?"

A laugh bubbles out of me at how serious he is with his request. "Yeah, I can do that."

"Good. Let's go, then. I have a surprise for you. Don't forget your jacket."

I put the bouquet in the filled vase and place it on the counter. They really are a pretty color.

Grabbing my puffy winter coat from the hook by the door, I shove my keys, phone, and wallet into the pockets instead of carrying a purse, and lock the door behind me.

"You're not going to try and get me to tell you the surprise?"

"No." I shrug. "I like surprises and don't want to ruin it. But I am curious as to how you knew where I lived."

"That's easy." He grins. "I can find out anything I want if I put my mind to it."

"Is that so?"

"Yes. Plus, my cousin Stefano can hack anything and

find out everything."

"Does that mean you already know everything about me?"

"No. I didn't ask him for anything other than the pertinent information I needed. Your address and phone number."

I raise my chin defiantly. "Good."

"Do you have secrets you're afraid I'll find out?"

"You already know my biggest one. I showed you my hand last night."

He places his hand over his heart. "I'm honored. But you know I saw a lot more than just your hand last night." He smirks. "A lot more."

I feel my cheeks heat and I look down at the floor.

"There's that pretty pink color again. Looks good on your face, too."

He needs to stop the flattery before I tell him to forget the date and to take me back upstairs and strip me bare to see me flush pink all over.

Luckily, the cold evening air cools my face when we get outside. Vinny steps up to the car parked right outside my building, but I don't think I can call it just a car. It's sleek, shiny, and looks like it would be fun to drive. "This is your car?"

"Yes, she is."

"She?"

"Her name is Ruby and she likes when I open her up and go fast." He winks, and I roll my eyes.

"I'll bet she does. But there's something to be said about

going slow and savoring the drive, too. But going fast is fun, too."

Vinny opens the passenger door for me with a smile. "I'll keep that in mind."

"What kind of car is she?" I ask him when we're both inside.

"A Mercedes AMG GT Coup."

"In ruby red?"

"Yeah, I wasn't too original when it came to naming her, I guess. But if you ever decide you want to christen her, I'll rename her after you."

"What an offer." I laugh. "I'll think about it."

"Now I'm thinking about it, so you better distract me."

I could say the same thing. The car may be on the smaller side, but I'm more than certain we could figure out a whole slew of things to get up to in here.

"You said you run The Aces with your cousin. Why don't you and your brother run it?"

"My brother prefers New York, while I've always loved this town. My sister loves the city too, but my cousin Alec and I prefer it here. I'm second to him, and we prefer our own little empire on the Jersey Shore to the chaos of the city."

"I'm not a fan of New York, either. There are too many people, it's dirty, expensive, and there's no quiet. The casinos never sleep here, but you can still find quiet."

"That's why when I graduated high school, I came right down here to learn the business with Alec and my dad."

"Oh, so it's not just you and Alec? Your dad is here

too?"

"No, he, uh…" Vinny scratches his jaw. "He died six, almost seven, years ago."

"I'm so sorry, Vinny."

"Thank you." He nods solemnly. "He was killed alongside my uncle, Alec's dad, in the city."

"Oh, I, uh… I'm sorry, I don't know what to say to that."

"It's okay." He shrugs. "It is what it is. It comes with being a Carfano. We have stricter security protocols in place now because of it."

"So, death is just imminent in your family?"

"We all have to go sometime."

"Yes, but most like to avoid it until they're old and have already lived a long, full life."

"I can assure you, I plan on doing that." He looks over at me. "How else do you think I'll be able to keep you happy? I have to be alive for that."

"What?" The word is barely audible, but Vinny hears me.

His eyes shift to mine and then back to the road. "You heard me."

I clear my throat, needing to change the subject. "You have a sister?"

"I do. Mia." He smiles when he says her name and I can tell he really cares for her. He doesn't offer anything else about her though, because a few seconds later, he's pulling into The Aces underground garage and stopping at a solid black gate. He punches in a code and the gate rises slowly to reveal another part of the garage that must be for just the family.

It's filled with beautiful cars. Classics, a few motorcycles, and more sleek sports cars like the one we're in. There's also a row of blacked-out Range Rovers like the one he drove me to the hospital in.

"This is quite a collection," I say, looking around.

"We like cars," he replies, as if it's such a normal thing to have a garage full of them to pick and choose from at a whim depending on your mood. "We have another level of cars in the garage at our building in the city, too."

"You said that so casually."

"I'm trying to impress you." He smiles. "This life isn't all about skirting death. We have fun, too."

"Why does it sound like you're giving me a sales pitch?"

"I just want you to see me, my life, and my family for who we are. Not through the lens of who you think we are."

"That's fair," I admit, and when he pulls into a spot and turns the car off, he reaches for my hand and brings it to his lips, kissing my knuckles softly.

"Wait right there," he tells me, climbing out of the car and coming around to open my door. He holds his hand out for me and I place mine in his, letting him help me out of the low seat.

"Such a gentleman."

"Sometimes." He winks, and I swear every time he does, my heart flutters like a damn butterfly taking flight.

Vinny places his hand on my lower back as we walk over to the elevator where he proceeds to put in a passcode, press his finger to a small pad, and then leans forward so a laser can scan his eye.

It must all be a part of the security updates he was talking about.

The elevator doors open, and when we step inside, Vinny presses the button labeled 'R', and we shoot up the entire building. The doors open again in a little vestibule area with nothing more than a black rug with The Aces' logo on it, a small table, and a potted plant.

He guides me out of the elevator and pushes the glass door open, causing a gust of frigid air to hit me in the face that renders me breathless for a moment.

"Wow, this is a great view." The Aces is the highest casino around, letting me see the lights of all the other casinos down the strip and the colorful lights of the pier's rides.

"That's why I brought you up here." The wind continues to whip at my face and I shove my hands deep in my jacket's pockets. "My apartment is only a few floors down and I love seeing the view from it every day. But there's more," he says, turning me away from the edge.

"Oh, my God. Wow," I breathe.

"We used to use the roof strictly as a helipad, but last year, Alec had that built for his girl, Tessa. Well, I guess his wife now." Vinny shakes his head. "I just found out they eloped when they found out she was pregnant."

"And you weren't invited?"

"That's what I asked too," he says, a sadness to his voice. "But they're happy, so I'm happy. I think they're going to throw a big party once they tell everyone. At least, I hope they do."

"That would be nice. Your family should celebrate both announcements."

"My thoughts exactly. Now, let me show you the inside."

This is freaking love.

His cousin built a whole damn greenhouse on the roof of the casino for his girl.

"It's made of a special kind of glass that can withstand the winds and weather this high up. Alec doesn't let anyone else inside besides the gardener that comes by to maintain the plants and Tessa, but I asked to borrow it for a special occasion."

"And I'm the special occasion?"

"Without a doubt, *dolcezza*."

Vinny opens the thick glass door for me and I'm immediately enveloped in warmth. There's a heater by the door and another on the other side, creating a comfortable temperature, and not a stifling one you usually find in greenhouses.

Lush green plants hang from the ceiling and line one of the glass walls on wooden stands and in planter boxes. The other side is lined with roses of all colors, but it's the really dark, nearly black ones, that draw my attention first. I walk over to them and touch the petals with my fingertips.

"These are beautiful."

"Alec had those created for Tessa by a botanist. I don't know the specifics, but it's a one-of-a-kind variety."

"That's so romantic."

"Don't say that in front of him. He'll deny it." Vinny

laughs, touching the pink roses nearby. They're the same color he brought me tonight.

"Is this where you got the roses?"

"No. Alec would kill me if I touched any of these." I want to think he's joking about that, but I don't think he is.

I finally take notice of the table set up for dinner and smile when he pulls the chair out for me. "Vinny, this is so nice. You didn't have to do this for me."

"That's where you're wrong. I absolutely had to, and will continue to. You deserve to be treated like you're special, because you are."

"Vinny." I look up at him through my lashes. "You need to stop saying all the right things."

"Not a chance, *dolcezza*." He taps me under my chin to get me to raise my gaze so he has a full view of my eyes. "And it's not just me saying shit to say shit. I mean every word. When I speak, it's the truth. I don't lie. Ever. You can ask my entire family if you want, but hearing me now, do you think I'm lying?" He asks seriously, his voice calm. "Has anything I've said to you since we met sounded like a lie?"

"No."

"Then let me say all the right things. Because they're all true."

"Okay," I whisper, my heightened emotions clogging my throat.

Vinny leans down and plants a soft kiss to my lips and hovers right above them for a few seconds. The centimeters of space are sparked like a live wire after a storm, bouncing all over the pavement, just waiting for something to come in contact with it so it can set it ablaze.

"I hope you're hungry," he rasps, the intensity of him holding back coming through.

"Starved," I tell him, and he groans, pressing his forehead to mine and closing his eyes.

"You're killing me, *bella*. If I kiss you how I want, I won't be able to stop, and I want you to know how fucking badly I want to know you." Kissing my lips quick, he straightens to tower over me. "And you said you'd give me your nice side. I wouldn't want to miss out on that."

Playful Vinny is back with a grin and a wink, and I exhale the breath I didn't know I was holding.

I'm so fucked with him.

CHAPTER 16

Vinny

I brought Lexi up here to show her that men who do bad things still have hearts.

We still feel.

We still care.

"This is delicious," Lexi praises, covering her mouth with her hand and taking a sip of the wine I just poured.

"It's from Carfanos."

"You have a restaurant?"

I nod. "Down in the casino. Best Italian in town."

I had an assortment of dishes brought up, not knowing what she likes or would be in the mood for.

Lexi's sampled the scallops, white fish, and veal, and I

love how unabashedly she eats and enjoys her food. I've gone on dates where the girl I'm with only eats a few forkfuls of lettuce, opting to drink wine instead.

Where's the fun in that?

I don't want to go on dates where I'm being watched as I finish my meal because she doesn't want to appear like she eats.

I know women can eat. My mom, aunts, sister, and cousins can pack away food like they're going into hibernation the next day, and I fucking love them for it. We're Italian. We like food.

"I think you're right. For dinner dishes, at least. Lunch, on the other hand, my grandfather wins."

"I have no problem agreeing with you there."

"Speaking of which, he says he owes you a soppressata sandwich and to come by any time."

"I'm not going to lie, I've thought about that sandwich every day since the club."

"Really?"

"Yes. But going to get one would have ruined my plan," I tell her, and she shakes her head.

"Are you trying to make me mad again?" she asks, but her lips are tilted up in a sly smile.

"No, not at all. In fact," I say, pouring more wine into both of our glasses. "I want you feeling even nicer." I smirk, loving the pink that stains her cheeks. "We still have dessert, too."

"Oooh, I'm ready for dessert," she says eagerly. "Good thing I left room for it."

I pull my phone out and send a message to Tessa's bodyguard, Tito, to bring it up. I've borrowed him for the night to help me with this dinner since he wasn't needed tonight and he's one of the few with the security clearance to access the roof.

"It'll be here in a few minutes."

"Well, until then…" she smiles, grabbing the plate of scallops. "These are too good to not finish. I mean, if you don't want them?" She bites her lip, her eyes begging me not to say I want them.

"Nope. All yours."

Her grateful smile is instant, and I think I just fell in love with her a little. She could give me that pleading look and I'd give her any damn thing. Literally anything.

And that, right there, is the start of it all.

I know it, and I'm surprisingly not scared of that fact.

"I've talked a little about my family with you, but I only know about Frank."

She looks reluctant at first, but then takes a sip of wine and dives right in. "It's just him and my mom now. My dad passed away when I was twelve and my grandmother when I was seventeen. Her and my grandfather were kind of star-crossed lovers who ran away to the states when she got pregnant with my dad. They couldn't have any more kids after him despite wanting a houseful, but they built a life full of love, laughter, and happiness that I'm happy to have been brought up in."

The wistful smile on her lips at the memories makes my heart twist, wishing I could say I had the same atmosphere growing up.

"Are you close with your mom?"

"We were. Sort of." She shrugs. "I was always closer to my dad and grandparents, and then after she got married a couple years ago, it hasn't been the same."

"You don't like her new husband?"

"No, he's fine. He takes care of her and I like that's she's happy again."

"But he's not your dad." I finish her unsaid thought and she nods. "Who taught you how to count cards?"

"Oh, that." She grins, her smile confident and proud. "I spent every day after school at the deli, doing my homework and helping out when I was done. My grandfather's local friends would come in and play cards or dominos, and they'd let me watch. I was determined to understand what the hell was going on." She laughs, sipping her wine. "Gin rummy was a favorite of theirs, but they taught me blackjack first since it was the easiest for a kid to understand. I was hooked, and I immediately needed to know how to win. Because, well…" she looks at me with a glint of mischief in her eyes. "I don't like to lose."

"Who does?"

"True. But I *really* hate losing. And the older men saw how frustrated I'd get when I couldn't control the cards to get what I wanted. So, one of them suggested I start using my brain to figure out my odds and learn to control the cards."

"How long did it take you?"

That twinkle in her eyes has me mesmerized. "I was determined," she says, and I laugh.

"I'm sure you were."

"My determination has paid my college tuition and then some, and now it's being used to help my family. I don't abuse it. That was the one rule my parents and nonno had as I was learning. They made me promise I wasn't to use it to simply steal money and get rich. They wanted me to find my own path in life and not have to rely on living a life where I'd spend my days in casinos and back rooms. That life either ends early or leads to a slippery slope of other vices I have no business indulging in. At least, that's what was said to me."

"They were right. It's a good rule. I've seen even the best gamblers fall at some point, and they don't recover from the hole they dig themselves into."

"I'm not greedy. I have everything I need."

"Do you?"

"Almost everything," she corrects softly, looking down into her wine glass. She looks back up at me through her lashes and it's a fucking punch to my gut.

Lexi's working her magic on me, but she doesn't know I'm already under her spell.

"What are you missing, *dolcezza?*"

"I'm not sure." The seduction in her voice is enough to make my cock throb painfully. "I'll see after dessert if you have it."

"Baby," I start to say, and she shakes her head.

"Not your baby."

Her eyes follow the spread of my lips as they curl into a slow grin, and they turn into those two blue flames I love to see burning when I lick my lips.

"We'll see about that."

Lexi finishes the scallops and takes a sip of wine. "That was really good. Thank you."

"You don't have to thank me. Seeing you smile and enjoy yourself is all the thanks I need."

"Alright, then," she says, placing her elbows on the table and her chin on her fists. She gives me a sweet smile that has my chest tightening and my dick hardening.

She has that way about her.

The ability to both make me feel more for her and make me want to fuck her.

It's a lethal combination, and one I've yet to experience with anyone but her.

I've wanted to fuck plenty of women, and have. And there was one woman, once upon my early twenties, that made my heart race whenever I was with her. But she was a liar, and everything I felt was a lie. Just like fucking those women was a bunch of lies. Well, not necessarily lies, but they were just fleeting releases I needed and then that was it.

I was forever chasing a feeling that was always gone too fast and left me feeling empty.

So far, it hasn't been that way with Lexi. I feel everything all at once with her and I desperately need to know if fucking her will be the same. I was desperate for more of her after simply being around her, and then I kissed her, and it was like a hit of cocaine – a rush to my system I had been missing out on. Then I tasted her pussy last night, and I need more.

I keep needing more pieces of her. I want them all, with my obsession only growing by the minute.

"If you keep giving me that beautiful smile, *dolcezza*, you're going to make me kiss it away. It's hard to resist you."

Her smile widens. "And if I don't want you to resist me?"

Her directness has my dick throbbing. "I don't know if I can stop at just kissing you, Lexi. I need you too damn badly. So, you probably shouldn't say that if you want me to behave. We still have dessert coming."

"No one's stopping you from having me," she says, and instead of calming me, she only revs me up more. "Certainly not me."

Lexi keeps her eyes on me as she stands, her lips tilted up in a mischievous grin that lets me know she's going to fulfill every fucking fantasy I have. I just hope she'll give me the time to make them all come true.

I turn towards her in my chair and she runs her hands up my chest and shoulders. "You have me twisted up, Vinny. You keep helping me when I don't want you to. You keep making me mad when you're being nice. And I don't think I can continue being mad at you for no real reason other than me trying to fight how I feel."

I cup her cheek. "Tell me how you feel."

"I like you."

I quirk my eyebrow and her eyes dance. "You do?"

"Yeah, I do. But it's more than that. After that first night, and every day since, I've felt crazy and unsteady, and it wasn't until you kissed me that I felt right again. But then my heart kicked into overdrive and the floor opened up to swallow me. You were there to keep me up though, so I didn't fall."

"And if I want you to fall?" I press, needing to know if she's as ready as I am to find out what happens when you let yourself feel without worrying if the other person is holding back.

"You'd let me fall?" she whispers, stepping between my spread legs.

"It wouldn't just be you."

A range of emotions pass through her eyes, and she slides her hands up my neck, rubbing her thumbs back and forth across my jaw.

Damn, her touch is a balm I want covering my body from head to toe.

"I don't know if I'm ready for that yet."

"Will you let me know when that changes?" She nods, and my heart fucking pounds like a bass drum. "Good. Now, let's have a taste of what it could be like."

I wrap my arm around her and pull her towards me. Her eyes change. The want and need in them shining bright.

"I think you need to take me down to your apartment, Vinny."

"And I think you need to let me taste those lips of yours *before* I take you downstairs, peel those sexy as fuck leather pants down your body, taste your sweet pussy, and then fuck you until you're screaming my name and coming all over my cock."

"Vinny," she whispers, a moan catching in her throat.

"Lexi," I whisper back.

Her eyes close and her lips fall to mine, her hands sliding

to the back of my head straight away.

I pull her even closer, lifting her so she'll climb onto my lap and straddle me. My hands find their way under her sweater and up her back to feel her heated skin.

Lexi moans at my touch, her body melting against mine like it's her undoing. And when her hips roll against me, it's *my* undoing.

Growling, I nip her bottom lip and she gasps, pressing herself down on me, which has both of us moaning into the other.

I deepen the kiss, my tongue delving into her mouth, tasting the wine still on her tongue. I could get drunk on her alone.

The fact that she's not fighting me this time, but eagerly grinding her sweet pussy against me, solidifies my confidence in knowing this woman wants me just as badly and desperately as I want her. She feels it too. She fucking feels all of it.

I slide my hands down her back and under the skin-tight leather. With my hands on her luscious ass, I squeeze her soft flesh and press her down firmly on my cock, rocking her back and forth.

Fuck.

I need her.

But I need to stop before I come in my pants like a damn teenager.

"We need to stop, *dolcezza*," I say, out of breath.

"Why?" she asks, just as breathless as me.

"Because this is going to end prematurely if we don't."

She smiles against my mouth, kissing me again, and distracting me again.

"Lexi," I groan, using every ounce of willpower I have to slip my hands out of her tight pants and the comfort of her pillowy ass.

"It seems you're the one who can't take it this time," she teases, kissing the corner of my mouth before climbing off me.

She's unsteady for a moment, and then she backs around the table to her chair with a sexy little smirk on those addictive lips of hers.

"You're just a tease," I tell her, pressing the heel of my hand to my cock and adjusting myself the best I can.

Luckily, my phone buzzes in my inner jacket pocket, and I eagerly grab for it. It's a message from Tito telling me he left dessert on the table outside the elevator. "I'll be right back. Dessert is here."

"Perfect timing, I guess." She smiles.

Yes, it is.

Lexi really enjoys the game. I just hope she's ready for it to end tonight when I have her panting, moaning, and begging for me to fuck her while she's under me.

I grab the two plates, and when I come back, I see she's already moved the dinner plates to the empty garden table behind her to make room.

I place a plate with a variety of small chocolates in front of her, but Lexi is looking at me like she wants *me* for dessert. And when her eyes drop to the bulge of my cock straining against my pants, she licks her lips.

Fuck.

"If you keep looking at me like that, *dolcezza*, I'll have you on your knees with my cock shoved down your throat and swallowing my cum as your dessert instead."

Her lips part with a little gasp and her eyes shoot up to mine.

I'm not fucking around anymore.

Lexi picks up a chocolate and bites into it, moaning as she chews slowly, teasing me like the little minx she is. "I don't see you following through on that little threat, Vincenzo."

She used my full name. She's not fucking around anymore either.

"You don't think so?" I ask, and she shakes her head, popping the rest of the chocolate into her mouth and moaning again just to rile me up.

I push the plate away from her. "Stand up."

She looks at me with a quiet defiance, challenging me to see if I'll really follow through.

"You're mistaken if you think I'm not a man of my word. And you're mistaken if you think anything about my threat is little. Stand. Up."

Lexi rises slowly, but even at her full height, she only comes up to my shoulders, so she still has to look up at me.

I grip her chin and tilt her head up further, leaning down so I'm just a breath away. "Get on your knees, Alexis."

She only hesitates for a moment before she lowers herself down my body. I offer her a hand to steady herself as she kneels before me, and the moment I release her, she slides her hands up my legs to rub my cock through my pants.

Grunting, my jaw ticks as I hold back, remaining still so I can enjoy the show of my girl on her knees before me.

Lexi undoes the button of my pants and slides my zipper down. She pauses, feeling me through my pants again, and I grind my teeth.

"What are you waiting for? I want to see those sweet lips of yours wrapped around my cock and feel your throat close around me as you choke on me. I want to know everything that hot mouth of yours is capable of when you're not giving me sass."

Lexi rubs her thighs together and it takes everything in me to not hoist her over my shoulder and carry her down to my bed to fuck her senseless.

She's turned on by the idea of choking on my cock, and if I didn't already think she was perfect, I know she is now.

Lexi bites her lip, and I shudder when she reaches inside my pants and her small hand wraps around my cock.

"Fuck," I grunt, and her eyes shoot up to clash with mine. She knows she's got me. I can see it. She knows she's in control and she fucking loves it. And I fucking love seeing her embrace her power.

Lexi pulls me from the restricting confines of my pants and she gasps when I spring free, which has me grinning and tracing my finger along her jaw.

"Open up, *dolcezza*." I tap the side of her mouth and she shakes her head, opting to run her fingers along my length first.

Lexi grips me at the base and runs her tongue up the underside of my cock, keeping her eyes on me to see my reaction.

Holy fuck.

I can't even think straight.

"You teasing me?"

She shakes her head no, but then proceeds to rim the tip of my cock with her tongue, making my vision blur and my head spin.

She's going to ruin me, and I'm going to let her.

Just before I'm about to lose my mind and think she's never going to give me what I want, Lexi throws me a sexy little wink and opens wide, taking me deep inside her mouth.

"Fuuuckk," I groan, my hand finding its way into her hair.

Lexi's tongue wields her magic as she bobs up and down my length, taking more of me each time while she gets used to my size.

I try and let her run the show, but when she sucks me like a goddamn vacuum, I lose control and thrust my hips forward, making her take me to the back of her throat. And just like I wanted, she chokes on me, those beautiful blue eyes watering.

I grip her hair tighter and pull her off my cock so she can breathe, but she grips the back of my thigh with her free hand and takes me back inside her hot mouth.

"You like sucking my cock, *dolcezza?*" I ask, and she hums her agreement. "Fuck. Do that again," I demand, and she does, the vibrations traveling through me like a bolt of lightning.

"You take me so good, baby," I praise, and she digs the pads of her fingers into my thigh harder, grunting her protest. "Sorry, baby, I can't hear you. Your mouth is a little busy with my cock to argue with me." I thrust my hips forward and her throat reflexively closes around me. "What was that?" I tease, and her watery eyes narrow. "If you want to argue, you better get to work." I wink, and she squeezes her hand around my cock, doing just as I wanted her to.

I know I won't last much longer. I've spent the past two weeks dreaming of her mouth on me and had her grinding on my lap just minutes ago.

Now I'm looking down at a goddess on her knees with my cock disappearing in and out of her mouth, and it's more than I can take.

I suck in air through my clenched teeth and groan when she does a swirl of her tongue around my head before plunging back down on my cock.

"Lexi."

My grip on her hair tightens and fire licks down my spine before I explode – shooting my cum down her throat.

Lexi groans and so do I. My soul leaves my body and she swallows it.

My grip loosens on her and she licks me clean before sitting back on her heels to lick her lips.

My girl can give head like a goddamn pro, and I'm not going to think about who taught her. If she gives me a name, I'd be too tempted to have him killed for knowing what having Lexi's mouth on him is like. Because if I have a say in our future, she's never going to suck a cock that isn't mine ever again.

She's all mine now.

I hold my hand out for her and she takes it to stand. I run my fingertips across her cheek and down her jaw, rubbing my thumb over her bottom lip.

I lean down to kiss her soft lips, but when I'm an inch away, she whispers, "Still not your baby."

Growling, I slam my mouth down on hers and kiss her until she's pliant in my arms. When I pull away, she blinks up at me, forgetting her argument.

I like my girl when she's feisty, but I also like her like this – too turned on and out of it to know what to say.

"Do you still want dessert?" I ask, leaning my forehead against hers.

"What?" she breathes, confused for a moment. "Oh, yes, I do."

Smiling, I tuck myself back in my pants and we sit down again. I reach for my wine and down the rest in my glass while Lexi takes a bite into another chocolate, moaning again.

She really is trying to kill me.

CHAPTER 17
Lexi

I bite into a chocolate and the hazelnut cream filling melts on my tongue. Moaning, I lick my lips to make sure I don't miss a single morsel, and Vinny's eyes darken. "These are amazing," I tell him. "You should have one."

He grabs one from his plate and pops it in his mouth. "Oh shit, this is good," he says, and I laugh. "But not as good as I know your soaking wet pussy would taste right about now."

Oh, my…

I swallow hard and grab my water, chugging it for my suddenly dry mouth and throat.

Vinny smirks and leans back in his chair, biting into

another chocolate. "Mmm," he hums, and I can feel the vibrations pulsing in my pussy as if he were doing it against me.

He pulls the candy away from his lips and puts on a show for me. His tongue darts out and delves into the halved chocolate, scooping the soft center out.

I'm dizzy.

"Mmm," he hums again, my clit throbbing. "It just melts on your tongue, doesn't it?"

My eyes are on his mouth, watching him swirl his tongue inside the now hollow chocolate. And when he jiggles it in and out, I can't help the little moan that leaves me.

Vinny smirks. "Am I distracting you?" he asks in a deep, seductive voice that has me reaching for my water again.

"Yes," I hiss, narrowing my eyes.

Two can play this game.

I still have two chocolates left, so I reach for the rectangular shaped one and bring it to my lips. Now it's his turn to narrow his eyes.

I run my tongue along the length of it and smile when he pops the rest of the chocolate he was teasing me with into his mouth. His attention is now fully on me.

I suck the end of it, humming my approval, and Vinny adjusts himself in his chair. But since I already gave him the real thing, I just give him a sweet smile and pop the whole thing in my mouth.

"See? Tease," he growls.

"I'd argue that now you're the tease."

"Oh, Lexi, I wasn't teasing you. It's what I'm going to do

to your pussy in a few minutes." He winks. "Are you finished with dessert?"

"Yes," I say quickly, and Vinny's smile is both smug and excited, and I'm struck with a pang in my chest that radiates through me in an echo that has every nerve ending in me on high-alert.

Vinny stands and holds my jacket up to help me put it on before holding his hand out for me to take. I slip mine in his and he immediately engulfs me in his warm embrace.

It feels safe.

I feel safe.

Like he's going to take care of me, in every sense of the phrase.

"Should we clean up?" I ask, looking back over my shoulder at the tables of dishes.

"No. Someone will come up and do it."

"Alright." I look around the gorgeous greenhouse one more time before stepping back out into the cold night air, and Vinny notices.

"I can bring you back anytime you'd like."

"Really?"

"Of course. I'd never deny you something that puts a smile on your face."

"You're being too nice," I tell him before I can stop myself.

"You're right," he says when we reach the elevator, and he pins me against the wall beside it, his mouth molding to mine in a kiss that has me losing my breath and causes every thought to fly out of my head.

Vinny grips my ass and lifts me, giving me no choice but to wrap my legs around his waist as he walks us into the elevator car.

My back hits the wall with a dull thud that only deepens our kiss when our mouths smash together.

I slice my fingers through his hair and grip the ends, making him groan into my mouth. It's sexy, and hot, and I want to feel him do it when his mouth is between my legs.

Vinny spins me around to another wall and tears his lips away to do his elevator security bullshit, and I bury my face in his neck – inhaling his masculine scent that's like warm vanilla and cinnamon. It has me licking his skin to see if he tastes as good as he smells.

Vinny slaps my ass. "It's not your turn to have a taste. It's mine."

His lips are on mine again, and it's a good thing the elevator ride is so short, because I have zero patience.

Vinny strides out of the elevator and down a short hall where he holds me with one hand to open his door. The second we're inside, he kicks the door closed and practically jogs through his apartment to his bedroom, where he bends forward to lay me down.

Vinny takes off his winter coat and suit jacket, and then makes quick work of my jacket and sweater, but pauses to look at me in just my leather leggings and bra.

The way he's looking at me...

Like I'm a tasty meal he can't wait to devour, and my core clenches.

I've never had a man look at me so brazenly. Vinny isn't

afraid to voice or show how much he wants me. I'm not used to that level of confidence and assuredness, and it scares me how much I like it.

"Let me taste these first," he says, unhooking my bra and slowly pulling it away from my body. His eyes light up like a kid on Christmas morning opening a gift he's been waiting all year for.

The cool air of his room hits my already hard nipples and they pucker into tight peaks.

"Fuck, Lexi," he groans, licking his lips.

He cups them in his large hands, rubbing his thumbs over my nipples. My head falls back on a moan that turns into a cry when he pinches them.

"I love hearing your sounds, *dolcezza*," he rasps in my ear before kissing his way down my neck and chest.

He drags his lips around my nipples, but doesn't touch them. "Vinny," I plead, thrusting my chest forward.

"Hmm?" he hums against me, continuing to circle around where I need him most, now with his tongue.

"Please," I beg. "I need…"

"What do you need?" He bites the side of my breast. "Is this not what you need?" I hear the teasing tone of his words and I get even more frustrated.

"No," I huff, and he chuckles, knowing he has me where he wants me.

"Is this better?" Vinny's hot mouth clasps around one of my nipples and I let out a raw scream, the sensation too much.

The sharp pain morphs into bolts of lightning spiking

through me with every suck and swirl of his tongue, and I'm left to melt into the bed, unable to stop the sounds coming from me.

"There's my music," he muses, paying equal attention to my other nipple – starting the whole deliciously painful process all over again.

I'm squirming beneath him as he kisses his way down my stomach, pausing to swirl his tongue around my belly button, which only has me squirming more.

"Ticklish?" He smirks, looking up at me with fire in his eyes.

I shake my head. "No. I just need you to keep going."

"Wasn't planning on stopping."

Vinny lifts my legs up one at a time to unzip my booties and drop them to the soft carpet at the foot of the bed.

He pauses to rake his eyes over me before he slowly peels my leather leggings down my legs, with every inch of skin he exposes turning flaming hot with my need for him to touch me.

Vinny tosses them on top of my discarded clothes, and in just my thong now, his heated gaze zeros in on the scrap of lace keeping me from being completely naked.

His eyes finally continue up my torso and then clash with mine. "It feels like I've waited two lifetimes for you."

My heart twists. I'm starting to feel the same. "I'm right here," I whisper, and his gaze darkens as he runs his hands up my outer thighs like he's making sure I really am.

Vinny taps my knees. "Open for me," he says, and the soft way he does has me obeying without hesitation.

The fight in me is gone.

I want him to take control.

I want him to fulfill every promise his eyes first offered me when we met that night in the club.

I want it all.

Vinny groans. "You're already so wet. The lace is clinging to your pussy." Bending down, he runs his nose up my inner thigh, and my legs reflexively open wider. "*Dolcezza*," he says, his nose running up the lace. "It's time for my dessert."

He plants a kiss to my bare skin right above my thong and then rips the lace from me in a single snap. I gasp at the sting and he gives me another kiss, looking up at me from between my hips.

"Don't hold back on those sounds," he says with a wink and tweak of my nipple – eliciting a moan just as he intended.

Vinny's hot tongue runs down the sides of my lips and he presses my legs flat to the bed to open me as wide as possible.

"You're addictive, *dolcezza*. I'm going to need you for dessert every night." He punctuates his statement with a long pass of his tongue up my pussy. "I'm going to see how fast I can make you come. Because if I don't get inside of you soon, I'm going to lose my goddamn mind."

"Please," I beg, agreeing completely, and Vinny stops teasing me and dives right in, using everything in his arsenal to get me to come in less than a minute.

Standing over me, his eyes eat up every inch of my body. "Fucking beautiful. You flush that pretty pink all over when you come."

I'm too lost to use my words, so I offer him a small smile and watch as he takes off his clothes. I can't wait to see what he has beneath that suit of his. I've felt how solid and strong he is, but I want to see every muscle and inch of golden skin that makes him that way.

He shrugs his shirt from his shoulders and my mouth waters. I'm speechless.

He's a work of art.

He's not ripped like he spends every spare moment working out, but he is defined and sculpted into a perfect specimen.

I swirl my eyes around his torso, eagerly awaiting the reveal of the rest of him as he undoes his pants and pushes them down. He steps out of them and my eyes zero in on his cock that's pointing right at me – long and thick.

Vinny wraps his hand around himself and strokes his length. "Alexis."

He says my full name and my eyes are pulled up to his. There's a seriousness to them that has me swallowing a lump of emotions I don't want to deal with right now. I just want to feel good. And while Vinny does make me feel good, he's also made it clear that he wants more with me, and I don't know how much of *more* I can give him right now.

He must see it in my eyes because he doesn't say anything aside from my name.

Grabbing my ankles, Vinny pushes me up until my head reaches the pillows and then climbs onto the bed. He grips me behind my knees and presses them up and out to the sides of my chest.

"You're so fucking beautiful spread open for me, *dolcezza*. I can't wait to see how beautiful you look with my cock inside you."

"Vinny," I moan, arching towards him. But the way he's holding me down restricts me. He positions himself at my entrance and I bite my lip, anticipating how good it's going to feel to have him stretching and filling me.

"You're leaking for me," he says, mesmerized.

"Vinny," I pant, my body hot. "Condom."

"Fuck," he curses, quickly reaching over to the bedside table and pulling one out. I watch him roll it down his length and he repositions himself at my entrance, the broad head of his cock pressing at me.

"I want to savor this, Lexi, but I don't think I can hold back this first time. I can't promise to be gentle and careful with you like you deserve."

"What I deserve is to be fucked until I can't remember my own name."

Vinny's eyes darken and his grip on the backs of my thighs tightens. "You sure you can handle that?"

"Anything you want to do, I can handle."

"*Cazzo, piccola, mi ucciderai.*" The Italian words spilling from his lips has me wanting to ask what he just said, but I don't get the chance. Vinny thrusts forward, burying himself inside me in one push.

I can't breathe.

I can't scream.

I can't do anything but feel my body burning and

splitting in two.

It's painful at first, but that quickly morphs into a blazing pleasure that blooms out to every fiber of my body.

"So tight, baby. You're strangling me. *Fuck*."

Vinny stills in me for a moment and then he pulls out slowly, the drag out making me feel every inch of him.

The moan that leaves me is deep and throaty, and I grip the comforter on either side of me, trying to ground myself.

"You feel so good, baby." He spreads me wider and thrusts back inside. "So fucking good."

Vinny turns wild and fucks me hard and fast.

He has me pinned where he wants me and it's so good, but I need more.

I need…

I don't know what I need, but I need more.

Vinny takes my ankles and brings them up to his shoulders so my legs are pressed to his chest.

I cry out at the change of positions.

He feels bigger this way. He reaches deeper.

"Fuck. You're even tighter like this." Vinny picks up the pace, each thrust hitting the knot deep inside me I've had twisting up since meeting him.

I cry out with each hit to it, and the slapping of our bodies coming together is erotic and dirty.

"Oh, fuck, yes," he hisses. "Yes, baby. Play with your tits for me."

I palm my breasts, squeezing and pushing them up towards my chin.

"Pinch your nipples like I would," he instructs, and I roll

them between my fingers, screaming out when a bolt of lightning strikes through me from my nipples to my clit and back. "Do it again, baby," he groans. "Squeeze me in that tight pussy of yours like you want me in there forever."

I do it again, and again, and Vinny growls like a feral animal, driving into me even harder.

My inner muscles start to flutter and I squeeze my nipples harder. "Vinny," I moan, and he smiles manically down at me.

"Yeah, baby?"

"I'm so close."

"I know," he says confidently. "You just need..." Vinny doesn't finish his sentence. Instead, he takes me behind my knees again and pushes them back to my chest and to the sides, and then presses down on my clit.

My vision blurs and my ears ring with my scream as my body explodes. I'm on fire and weightless, but I still feel Vinny slam into me one last time, splitting me open and releasing a guttural groan that brings my hearing back.

Wave after wave of pleasure flows over and through me, and my weightlessness turns heavy as I'm pulled under a current that doesn't want me to surface.

CHAPTER 18

Vinny

I look down at my girl coming apart at my doing and pride swells in my chest.

She's fucking magnificent.

Her body is flushed that pretty pink all over, and I look down where we're joined to see her pussy flushed a darker pink from the rush of blood flow, and I want to take a picture. I want to always have an image of our first time together, but I'd have to leave her to grab my phone, and I don't want to do that.

She feels too good.

Her pussy continues to pulse around me and I can't wait until she trusts me to fuck her with nothing between us. I want to feel her bare. I want to feel everything with her bare. Fucking cut me open and take all of me.

I start to rock in and out of her, slow and shallow, just to watch my cock move in and out of her. It's a sight I'm going to keep in my head forever.

Lexi whimpers and then moans, her hands falling from her perfect tits to her sides.

"Vinny." She moans my name as I rock, and she squeezes me again.

"Let me watch." Her eyes open lazily to look at what I am, and she mewls like a needy kitten, biting her lip. "You look so beautiful. You take my cock so well, baby."

"Yes," she sighs, and I swell inside her, needing to come again so soon. I don't rush it this time, and I keep my eyes on where we're joined.

I was blinded by all of her before, but now I'm focused on just this. Just us coming together and fitting so fucking perfectly.

I release one of her legs to rub slow circles around her already swollen clit at a pace that matches my thrusts, and Lexi moans loudly. I fucking love that sound, and it's because of me.

This pace would never have gotten me off before, but it only takes a few minutes for me to feel Lexi's inner muscles flutter around me and the slow fire to lick down my spine.

"Come for me again, *dolcezza*." She's followed instructions so well thus far, and she doesn't disappoint me now.

Her neck arches back and her eyes pinch closed. She

clamps down around me, milking my cock and pulling my orgasm from me a second time.

My deep groan mixes with hers, and this time I wish I had taped us. I want to listen to her. I want to see her. I want to relive this moment when she's not around.

I plant soft kisses on her chest and then her lips before I slowly pull out of her. She shudders at the loss of me, and I leave her for only a moment to discard of the condom and dampen a washcloth. Returning to the goddess in my bed, I clean her gently, loving how much cum I have to wipe up.

Lexi's eyes are already closed, and she makes soft mewling sounds while I take care of her.

Her dark hair is lost amongst my black sheets, and it makes me want to get a set of white ones so I can see it better next time she's in my bed.

I shift her around as I pull the comforter and sheets back, and join her beneath them, pulling her against me.

I twirl my fingers around the ends of her silky hair and she instinctively moves closer to me, hooking her leg over mine and draping her arm over my torso.

She's warm and naked and I need her even closer. I pull her fully on top of me and continue to play with her hair while I palm her ass with my other hand.

I let myself drift off – comfortable, content, and happy to hold my future against me.

CHAPTER 19
Vinny

Soft, warm lips against my chest pull me from a deep sleep where I was dreaming of the best sex of my life with the girl I can't get out of my head.

But when I blink my eyes open, I'm met with the prettiest blue ones that remind me of the Atlantic when the sun hits it. Dark around the edges but lighter going towards the middle, with veins of the dark blue slicing through.

"Hi," she whispers, a soft shyness to her.

"Hi," I whisper back, pulling her up to my lips so I can kiss her. "I thought I was dreaming, but it was my mind replaying everything we did."

Lexi is straddling my waist and I press my fingers into

her soft flesh. She bites her lip, but a soft moan still escapes them.

I keep massaging her ass, loving the way her eyes change when I do. When I feel her pussy grow wet against my lower stomach, I pause, reaching between her from behind to feel for myself.

"Fuck, baby, you're already wet and I wasn't even trying."

"I can't help it," she says, and my cock that was already hard from my dream, now stands at full attention, needing her attention.

I groan and spread her cheeks apart, tilting her pelvis downward so I can feel her pussy right against me.

"Vinny," she whispers against my lips, sinking her teeth into my lower lip. "I'm a little sore, but please, I need more."

I don't need her to ask me twice.

Her wet pussy makes it easy for me to slide her down my torso until my cock is nestled between her ass cheeks. I press them together to swallow my cock between her two globes, and we both groan.

Lexi's eyes turn molten.

"Let me do the work, baby. Just feel."

She nods against my chest and I fall for her a little more. She's stopped fighting me when I call her baby, and she's given me her trust to take care of her.

The honor isn't lost on me.

Her trust isn't lost on me.

With my hands gripping her ass, I tilt her hips back and run her up and down my length so she coats my cock with her juices, and then plaster myself between her cheeks again.

I've always wanted to do this and Lexi has the perfect ass for it.

Her breathing is ragged against my chest and her hands slide around me to hook under my arms and grip my shoulder blades.

She's clinging to me like I'm her lifeline, and when I look down her back and see the way her spine arches back to meet her ass, and the way her ass is swallowing my cock, I grip her harder, needing her as my lifeline, too.

I move her against me, and on every down stroke, I grind her clit against me. She's whimpering and moaning, and I know she's close.

"Come with me, Lexi," I murmur, and she nods, digging her nails into my back. I move her up and down twice more and then tell her, "Now." I push her down as I thrust up and she cries out, her pussy flooding the base of my cock as I explode, coming all over the top of her ass.

I release her cheeks from my grip and massage them until we both drift off again.

I wake to Lexi trying to move off me, but I tighten my arm banded around her and pat her ass.

"What are you doing? I'm comfortable."

"Me too," she agrees. "But I need to use the bathroom."

"Fine," I sigh, releasing her.

Lexi scrambles off the bed and I bend my arm behind

my head to give myself a better view of her walking away.

It's been a long time since I've woken with a woman in my arms and in my bed that I didn't already have an exit plan for.

I don't want Lexi to leave, though. I don't want us to leave my bed for at least a day.

She returns to me and the shy look on her face has me grinning.

"What?" she asks.

"I was just thinking about how I don't want us to leave my bed for at least a day. Maybe two. And when we do, it'll only be to get water and food to refuel."

"Vinny," she says on a laugh, that beautiful smile wiping away her shyness. "We can't have sex for days on end. I don't think I could take it."

"You would take it, and you would love it." I smile, making her laugh again.

"Alright, well, we can't test that theory today. I need to go home and change and then head to the deli. We're packing up anything that won't last through the closure and bringing it to the nearest shelter."

"Would you like my help?"

"Oh," she says, surprised. "Would you like to help?"

"Yeah, I would."

"Then yes, I'd like your help."

"Good. But I think we need to shower first." I hop out of bed and walk her back into the bathroom. "And I fully plan on getting a little dirty with you before I clean you."

Kissing the side of her neck, I turn the shower on and drag her under the hot stream of water.

CHAPTER 20

Lexi

"I'll meet you there?" I ask Vinny, back in my apartment after I've changed clothes.

"Why?"

"I don't know. It might raise questions about why I'm arriving with you in the morning."

He looks surprised, but smiles. "Are you ashamed to be seen with me the morning after? Wow, I feel cheap, Alexis Manzato."

"You should," I tease. "I got what I wanted from you, so now you can go."

For a moment, I think he believes I'm serious because his smile fades just the slightest and his eyes flicker with something too quick for me to catch. But then it's gone, and his cocky grin is back.

"That's funny." He steps up to me and cages me against my kitchen counter. "Because I recall you asking me for more, and trust me when I say I have plenty more to give you. So, you might not want to be so quick to cast me aside."

"Alright. I'll give you a little more time." I smile, running my hands up his chest and around his neck.

"How kind of you," he says sarcastically, using his lips to quiet me from any further smart remarks.

His kisses are addictive.

He has a way of clearing every thought from my brain aside from him, and always leaves me wanting more.

"We should go, unless you want to explain to your grandfather why you're going to be a few hours late."

"Fine," I sigh, and he smiles against my lips, kissing me quick before releasing me from the cage of his strong arms.

"We can drive separately if you'd like," he finally agrees. "This time, at least."

Vinny walks me down to my car, and on my way to the deli, I look in my rearview mirror and see his car right behind me. I like that he was taken aback when I said I wanted to drive separately. I think I'm throwing him for a loop with him seemingly all-in and I'm still trying to hold off from being completely irrational.

I know if I let him into every thought, feeling, function, and decision I make, then I'll never be able to untangle myself from him. There's no coming back or saving me after that.

I'm also not entirely sure I can trust him yet to do that.

He's a Carfano.

He's in the mafia.

His life is woven into all things illegal and looked down upon by society.

He's probably killed a man. Or many.

He runs Atlantic City with his cousin, and there's no way they can do that without getting their hands dirty.

I have to be the one to decide if I can live with that.

Parking around the back of the building, I sit there for a moment and take a deep breath. I'm overthinking this. I just had a blissful night with him – the best I've ever had – and here I am, ruining it with all the what ifs and negative possibilities that might never be.

I need to just live in the moment and take whatever Vinny and I are day by day.

A knock on my window startles me out of my thoughts and Vinny opens my door for me. "You okay?"

"Yes. I was just thinking."

"About me?"

"Yes, actually," I admit.

"Can I ask what about?"

I give him a small smile. "No, you cannot."

"Alright. But you know, one day you're going to share what's going on in that gorgeous head of yours with me."

"Am I?"

"Yes, you are."

Placing my hand on his shoulder, I lift up on my toes and give him a soft kiss. "I'll tell you that one of my thoughts was how last night was the best of my life. Everything about it was perfect."

"For me, too."

"Really?"

"Yes, *dolcezza*. It may surprise you, but I'm not a heartless man. And last night, I felt it all with you. I'm glad you did, too."

"I know you're not heartless," I tell him, placing my other hand over his heart to feel it beating strongly under my palm.

Vinny kisses me long and slow, and I forget where we are for a minute. "Let's go inside before I toss you in my car and take you back to my place."

"Oh, right, inside. Yes."

My flustered answer has Vinny grinning from ear to ear, and I huff out a lungful of air, needing to regain my composure to be around my nonno and not give away the fact that Vinny spent the night fucking me like he owned me.

Vinny holds the back door open for me and I hear nonno puttering in the kitchen. "Hey, nonno!" I yell out, and he pops his head out from the kitchen.

"Good morning, my dear. Oh, Vincenzo, good morning to you, too," he adds, coming out to shake his hand.

"Good morning, Frank. Lexi told me you're packaging up food for the shelter, and I'm here to help any way I can."

"I won't turn away the help. Alexis already does too much for me."

"Nonno, you know I don't mind helping."

"I know, but now you don't have to lift anything heavy

today."

Vinny laughs. "I'm great at lifting heavy things."

Vinny and my nonno have been acting like old friends all morning. Vinny said something in Italian, and once nonno learned he spoke the language, all bets were off. I only know a little Italian, so I'm not entirely sure what they've been saying, but seeing them smile and laugh together…it stirs something in me.

I can see them having long talks and sipping wine while my nonno cooks Sunday dinner. I can see Vinny coming to help me at the deli and seeing it as fun and not some burden he feels he has to do to get me to like him.

I just packed a box of things to stock nonno's fridge with, and when I come back down, I pause in the hallway, hearing my name spoken.

"Do you like my granddaughter, Vincenzo?"

"I do, sir. Very much."

"Good. If you haven't already figured it out yet, she's a strong and independent young lady. But she needs someone to take that burden I know she feels."

"I only want to make her life easier. You can trust me on that."

"I saw the way you've been watching her today, and the way she's been watching you when you're not looking. I see. I know. It's the beginning of something big, Vincenzo."

"I'm hoping for that, Frank," Vinny says, and I can hear

the actual hope in his voice.

He thinks we're at the beginning of something big?

"And since I want this to be the start of something big, I want to apologize to you, Frank."

"What for?"

"I was trying to get Lexi's attention by inserting my help where it turns out it wasn't needed, and I unknowingly insulted you in the process. My help was never driven from a place where I thought the deli needed to be something different to succeed, and the last thing I wanted was for you to feel like I was insulting you. I was just trying to get Lexi to see that I was a nice guy."

"Thank you. I appreciate you telling me. Alexis said as much, but I see now you're a sincere man, Vincenzo."

"I try my best to be, sir."

"I may not like to admit it, but I'm not getting any younger. My work is my life. It's my home. But I know change is needed. Especially if I want to remain in business."

"Lexi won't let anything happen to the deli, Frank. I know she loves it as much as you do."

"She does." I hear the smile in my nonno's voice. "I don't know what I'd do without her."

"I hope neither of us has to ever find out."

I think my heart is going to explode in my chest. Hearing them talk about me like that… I feel seen and cared for, and if I eavesdrop anymore, I may just not be able to handle it.

"Alright, nonno, I put all the food away upstairs," I say, coming around the corner. They both look over at me from the table they're sitting at, and I stop short, playing dumb like I didn't hear anything. "What?"

"Nothing. We were just talking about lunch. Soppressatas all around?"

"Will you tell me what's in that spicy red pepper spread yet?" Vinny asks, and nonno shrugs.

"Maybe one day. If you take care of my Alexis, then I'll consider it."

"Nonno!"

"Deal," Vinny says, and they shake on it.

"Are you serious?" I ask, putting my hand on my hip. "You're trading me for a sandwich spread?"

"Not trading," Vinny says with a smile. "Just negotiating."

"That's not much better. But I'll get them started if you two need more time with whatever is happening here," I joke, waving my hand between them.

"No, no, you sit and have a rest," nonno says, vacating his seat for me. "I'll make them."

"If you're sure."

"I am."

He disappears into the kitchen and I take his seat. "He likes you," I tell Vinny.

"What's not to like?" His cocky grin has my core clenching, and I roll my eyes, honestly not able to come up with an answer to that. "Exactly." He winks, and I narrow my eyes. "Save that feistiness for later, *dolcezza*."

My core clenches again and my panties dampen.

Dammit.

CHAPTER 21
Vinny

I had the best night of my life with my girl last night, and a good morning and afternoon with her and Frank. He's a great man, and I think I won him over today. I was able to dust off my Italian, which I noticed made Lexi smile. I'll speak Italian all damn day if she wants so she'll smile at me like that.

I had to learn it growing up because my grandfather always told us that it was important to know and remember where we came from. And if we were going to be Carfanos, then we had to speak like the Carfanos before us.

I thought it was pointless as a kid, but grew to appreciate it. It's come in handy when we want to talk business in a situation that isn't exactly private, and now I can use it to impress my girl.

My phone buzzes on my desk and I pick it up when I see who it is. "Hey, Carthwright, do you have news for me?"

"Yeah, we got a lead on Pastorelli. He got in a bar fight last night, but bolted before cops arrived. He was identified by the bartender."

"Which bar?"

"O'Conner's."

"I know it."

"The bartender also said he's a regular."

"Good to know. If you get anymore leads, let me know."

"You too."

Carthwright just gave me the only lead I need.

I go next door and knock on Alec's door before walking right in. "Carthwright just called and said Pastorelli was in a bar fight last night at O'Connor's. They didn't get him, but the bartender said he's a regular."

"Are they going to sit on the place?"

"No, so I'm going to have two of our guys there every night until he returns. He hasn't left town yet, which means he's a creature of habit. I doubt he'll leave what he's comfortable with."

"Good. We need to get him before he ruins another business."

"Are you free for another date tonight, *dolcezza*?"

"Two in a row? You're not busy?"

"The only thing I'm going to be busy doing tonight is you, baby."

She bursts out laughing, and it's music to my ears. "Vinny!"

"What? I thought it was clever."

"It was. What did you have in mind for the date part of the evening?"

"I want to take you to dinner. There's a place on the water I think you'll like."

"I would like that."

"I'll pick you up at 7?"

"I'll be ready."

"Be ready to stay at my place, too."

"That's a bit presumptuous."

"Not really, baby. I'll see you soon."

Hanging up, I head up to my apartment with a smile, knowing my night is going to be occupied by a sexy goddess laid out naked in my bed.

I pull up to Lexi's apartment at exactly seven, and she steps out from the lobby doors. My heart races. She's so goddamn beautiful.

I don't understand how she hasn't been swept off her feet by someone else, but I've never been happier that she hasn't.

I open the passenger door for her and she gives me one

of her sweet smiles. "Thank you."

"You look beautiful, Lexi."

She leans up on her toes and gives me a soft kiss. "Thank you."

"Don't I look good, too?" I joke, winking.

"You know you do," she says, giving me another kiss before getting inside the car. "So, where are we going?" she asks when I get in and start the car.

"South Dockside. Have you ever been?"

"Yeah, it's so pretty there. But it's January."

"They have an inside section. But they also put heaters on the porch and decks."

"Oh, okay." She perks up, looking out the window as I make the short drive.

When we get there, the wind is whipping off the water, blowing Lexi's hair around her face. She laughs, her attempt at taming it a futile effort.

"Hold on." She reaches into her purse and pulls out a clip. I watch her, fascinated as she turns so the wind is at her face and she twists her hair up at the back of her head, securing it with the clip. "You're staring," she says with a grin.

"I know."

Her cheeks heat and I pull her close, placing my lips to her heated skin to feel it for myself. "You know I love that color on you."

Lexi and I head inside, and we're seated on the upper deck where there are standing heaters in each of the corners.

"What are you studying in school?" I ask her after we

place our orders.

"Psychology. I love learning how the brain works and how people work. The dynamics of relationships and friendships and people's behaviors in general is what fascinates me."

"Do you want to be a therapist?"

"Oh, no. Nothing like that. I went to college because it was a dream of my grandparents and parents. Growing up, all I ever wanted was to help my grandfather and work at the deli." I shrug, feeling kind of stupid. "Which is why I'm minoring in business. I know it's probably a waste of time to even go to college if I don't have a plan to use the degree, but..." I shrug again.

"No, it's not waste of time. If you were miserable and forcing yourself to get through all the classes and work because it was someone else's dream when you had no plans to use that degree, then I'd say it might be a waste of time. But not if you love it. I never got to go to college, and sometimes I wonder what it would've been like."

"I commute, so I just go to class and go home. I really don't know anything about the traditional college experience either. I mean, I've been to a few frat parties and hung out at the library to do research, but I think college is a lot different when you live in the dorms. But the thought of sharing a small room with a stranger was never on my list of things I wanted to do."

"You also wouldn't want to explain why you leave on the weekends looking like you're going to a party but come back with stacks of cash and smell of cigarettes. People would get the wrong idea." I wink, and she laughs.

"True. But people always get the wrong idea, anyhow."

"What do you mean?"

"Everyone assumes what they want about a person just by looking at them."

"You want to know what I assumed when I first saw you?"

"I don't know, do I?"

"I assumed you'd be the best thing that'd happen to me. And so far, my assumption has been correct."

"Vinny." She smiles. "That's sweet."

"I bet you didn't think I would be sweet when you first saw me. And you certainly didn't think I would be sweet when I told you who I am."

"Perhaps," she says, swirling her straw around her glass of water. "And perhaps I simply assumed you'd be amazing in bed."

My smile is instant. "Well, that assumption is warranted, *dolcezza*. And true."

She rolls her eyes. "Okay, don't get a big head over it."

"Can I get a big something else over it?"

"I'm hoping you do."

"Plan on it, baby."

Our food is dropped off and we eat and talk about the classes she's taking this semester. She has a presentation and a big paper due this week, so I'll have to remember not to be too needy with her time like I want to be.

"I'll be right back," she announces, pushing her chair back. "You can look at the dessert menu while I'm gone."

"I'm already looking at it," I say to myself, raking my eyes up and down her body.

"Are you finished, sir?" our waiter asks me when Lexi disappears inside.

"Yes, we are. Can I see your dessert menu?"

"Of course." He clears our plates and brings me a menu.

I peruse it quickly. "We'll have a chocolate mousse pie and two cannolis."

He nods and walks away, and Lexi comes back a few minutes later, angry and practically shaking.

"What's wrong?"

"He's here," she says in a rush.

"Who?"

"Ben. That fucker who robbed the deli. He's at the bar inside."

"You're sure it's him?"

"Of course I am. It's only been a couple weeks since I've seen him."

"Did he see you? You didn't confront him, did you?"

"No. I wanted to tell you first. I did contemplate swinging a full bottle of liquor at his head, but I held back. Should we call Detective Carthwright?"

I want to tell her no – that I'll take care of him – but I know I should. With him and his partner robbing other businesses, it changes things. If it was just Frank that he robbed, then I'd handle it with the family. But the neighborhood needs to know the thieves have been arrested and that they're safe again.

If we take care of the problem ourselves, then the

community won't know, and will still be weary and think they might be next. And I'm sure as hell not in the business of telling people when we take care of problems. Spreading that shit around is like painting a bullseye on our backs for people to look at us a little too closely.

"Yeah, I'll call him right now." Standing, I walk over to the railing where a table isn't occupied, and pull my phone out.

"Carthwright," he answers.

"It's Vinny. I'm at South Dockside and Pastorelli is here at the bar."

"He must've not wanted to go back to O'Connor's since the cops were called on him last night. I'll be there in ten."

"Thanks. I'm on the upper deck. Let me know when you've got him so he doesn't bolt when he sees who I'm with."

"Understood."

I head back over to the table and Lexi eagerly asks, "Is he coming?"

"He'll be here in ten."

"Good. Should we go down there to make sure he doesn't leave?"

"No, we're not going to do that. He'll recognize you and bolt. Carthwright will be here soon enough. Ben's not going anywhere."

"You better be right." Her eyes are telling me she's giving me a chance to have her trust and to not fuck it up.

"I am. You can trust me."

She doesn't respond to that, but rather bites into one of

the cannolis that was delivered while I was on the phone.

She still doesn't trust me fully, and while I want to be upset about it, I understand. Maybe this will help gain some from her.

CHAPTER 22

Lexi

Vinny says I can trust him, and I want to, but I'm going to blame him if Ben leaves before the detective gets here. It's already taken a couple weeks for anyone to find him. I don't want him slithering back into the hole he's been hiding in when he's so close.

I eat the delicious cannoli and half of the mini mousse pie, sliding the rest over to Vinny who gives me one of his smiles that warms my stomach. "You can have it," he tells me.

"I want to share with you. It's good."

"If you insist."

"I do."

"Let's hope this isn't the only sweet dessert you share with me tonight," he teases, and I can't help but smile.

"We'll see."

Vinny takes a spoonful of pie and then pulls his phone out. "He's been taken into custody."

"He has? I didn't hear any sirens."

"Carthwright's discrete."

"I see why you chose him to work for you."

"He doesn't work for me, per se. He's just a trusted detective that I can go to for information when needed."

"That's a nice way of putting it."

"It is, isn't it?" he grins, spooning the rest of the mousse pie into his mouth.

Pulling out his wallet, Vinny tosses a couple hundreds on the table and stands, holding his hand out for me to take. "I'm ready for my second dessert. See? I have a nice way of putting a lot things." He winks.

I take his hand and stand. "I know you do." Leaning up on my toes, I kiss his cheek and whisper in his ear, "But you know I don't like when you're too nice."

Vinny wraps his arm around my waist and practically drags me out of there. "You love teasing me when I can't have you right away, don't you?"

"Maybe I like seeing you get all wound up and brutish."

"Baby, I'll be a brute all you want. I'd love to lift you up and toss you around how I want you."

"Go ahead," I challenge, and he gives me a feral grin – an animal ready to catch its prey.

"Get in the car, Alexis," he orders, holding the door

open for me.

Vinny drives as fast as he can back to The Aces, and when we park in the garage, he rushes around to my side and opens my door. "Come on, baby," he says in a deep, sexy voice.

I take his hand and he pulls me out, only to drop down and lift me over his shoulder. "Ah! Vinny!"

He slaps my ass. "You told me not to be too nice. You can't take it back now."

I bounce on his shoulder as he walks to the elevator, and I grip the bottom of his jacket to keep steady.

"These jeans are painted on you," he murmurs, rubbing his palm over the globe of my ass. "But I wish you were wearing something more accessible for me." He runs his hand down the back of my thigh and up between my legs. "I could've gotten started early."

"I'll keep that in mind."

He slaps my ass again and I choke out a little yelp. That one stung, but it pools between my legs and I bite my lip. I wish he had easier access, too.

When we get inside his apartment, it's déjà vu from last night. He hurries down the hall, this time tossing me on top of his bed – all gentleness gone.

The air is whooshed out of me and Vinny smiles, that sexy predator/prey look back in his eyes.

He grabs my ankles and drags me back towards him. He's not gentle in the way he tugs and tears at my clothes until I'm naked and he's looking down at me still fully clothed.

"I want to see you, too," I tell him, propping myself up on my elbows. "You get to look at me like this," I say, sliding my left foot up towards me and then letting my leg fall to the side. "But I only get a few seconds to admire you before you're on me."

"That's the best part, *dolcezza.*" He smirks. "But, of course, if you want to look, I'll let you look."

Vinny takes his clothes off, and my eyes eat up every inch of skin he gives me until he's standing there like a museum piece I can study.

I bite my lip and take my time going over him. I lift my finger and make a circle motion in the air for him to turn around. He smiles and does as I wish.

Damn, he's got a nice ass.

And that back? Holy shit.

His muscles bulge and flex under his golden skin to show me the strength he hides under his suit and how he was able to so easily lift and carry me.

"You almost done ogling me, baby?"

"Almost. Keep turning," I instruct, and he listens, facing me again. His cock is hard and pointing right at me – the head swollen and leaking cum already.

I lick my lips and he groans. "You're leaking for me baby. I can see how wet you've grown from just looking at me, and it's the sexiest fucking thing in the world."

"You're leaking for me, too," I point out, and he smirks, gripping himself. "And if you don't put a condom on and get inside of me, I'm going to start without you."

"I'd love to see you touch yourself, baby, but I need

inside of you too fucking badly."

Vinny grabs a condom from the nightstand and sheaths himself. "I need to see your eyes when I slide into you, but then I'm going to flip you over and fuck you from behind with your ass in the air as you scream into the pillows."

"Please," I moan, letting my other knee fall to the side as an invitation.

He's on me in a second, the broad head of his cock at my entrance and his hand cupping my cheek. "Keep those eyes on me."

Vinny pushes into me and I watch as his eyes darken and turn to puddles of desire that are trying to see inside every corner of me.

When he's all the way inside of me, he pauses, brushing my lower lip with his thumb. "Ready for me to no longer be nice, baby?"

"Yes," I sigh. "Please."

He kisses me hard, grabbing my breasts in his hands and tweaking my nipples.

I yelp and he pulls back, grinning as he pulls out of me and slams back inside, all gentleness gone.

Ohmygod.

He fucks me hard, thrusting into me while he grips my breasts roughly, pinching my nipples every time he hits home, which elicits a cry from me each time.

"Let me see those eyes," he urges, and I peel them open to see his shining with too many emotions. Too many to read and too many to feel. "That's it. There they are. Let me see how you feel when I'm fucking you."

"Vinny," I moan, and he twists my nipples, sending shots of pain through me that turn to heat and pleasure, and make every nerve ending in me fire off with sparks.

With a growl, Vinny pulls out of me, grips my hips, flips me over like a rag dog, lifts my ass in the air, and thrusts back into me.

"Fuck," he barks, slapping my ass.

I turn my head to the side and gasp. "So big," I manage to say, and he slaps my ass again.

"That's right, baby. My big cock stretches and fills your tight pussy like I was made just for you. You take me so well. So beautiful." He runs his hands down my spine and around to knead my swaying breasts – the sensation completely different from when on my back.

Vinny rolls his hips and I squeeze around him, loving the feeling of him inside me so damn much.

Sliding his hands back down my spine and to each of my ass cheeks, he lifts and spreads them, tilting my hips back towards him.

"Put your hands out and brace yourself," is all the warning he gives me before he pulls out until just his tip is inside me, and then slams back inside. I put my hands against his padded fabric headboard just in time to keep me from being pushed up the bed, and I push back against him, meeting his every stroke.

"Yes, baby. So good," he groans. "Fuck me right back."

I let him push me up the bed a few inches with his powerful, hard thrusts, and I bend my elbows to give me the leverage I need to keep pushing back against him.

"I could fuck you forever, *dolcezza.*"

"Please," I beg, wanting that too. I don't want this feeling to end. I don't want to stop the intense connection.

"We have forever to fuck, but you're going to come for me when I say." I grunt into the pillows and he slaps my ass. "Got it?"

"Yes!" I cry out, and he slaps my other cheek.

Vinny pumps into me one, two, three more times.

"You're soaking my cock with your sweet cream. One day, I'm going to record it so you can see how fucking good we look coming together."

Oh…

The thought of that is so fucking hot.

"Yes," I moan.

"You'd let me?"

"Yes," I moan again, and he growls, gripping my ass harder.

"Fuck, yes, baby. Come for me." He slams into me even harder, the slapping of us joining making me wetter. "Now," he barks, and my pussy listens right away.

I scream into the pillows as I clamp down around him and Vinny lets out a low, guttural groan, and then collapses on top of me. His weight is a welcome relief. A comfort blanket covering me in his strength.

Kisses run down my spine and I arch into them, with goosebumps blooming across my skin where he presses his lips.

Vinny's spooning me from behind and he doesn't say anything. He just covers me in gentle kisses.

I hear him rip open a condom package, and then he lifts and hooks my leg back over his, pulling me down onto him as he thrusts up into me.

We both groan at the connection.

I reach back and grab Vinny's hand, bringing it around to cup my breast and squeeze it with him.

We rock against each other, finding our rhythm in a slow and deliciously drawn-out pace that lets me feel and savor every inch of him.

Vinny kisses across my shoulder and I stretch my neck to the side to give him more access.

Moaning, I bring our joined hands from my breast to between my legs, and I press the pad of his middle finger to my clit.

I shudder and he groans, circling my clit until my legs are shaking and my orgasm hits me without warning like a freight train barreling through me.

Pressed against Vinny, I feel his entire body shudder as he comes, pulling me even closer as I drift off again, loving the feeling of him still inside of me.

CHAPTER 23
Lexi

I've been super busy with school this week. I had a big paper due and I've been preparing for an oral report, which means I haven't had time to see Vinny since our date last weekend, and I've only been able to text him sporadically.

He said he understands, but for the first time, I'm wishing I wasn't in school so I could spend my spare time with him.

Oh, God.

For me to say that means I've moved past the keep my distance, guard my heart stage of all of this.

Vinny has managed to worm his way inside my head and heart, making more than just a little room for himself.

I've taken one too many breaks this past week to replay everything we did over the weekend, leaving me hot and bothered and needing to find my own relief before being able to focus on my work again.

My mind was definitely off Vinny when I talked to my mom today and I updated her on everything going on with the deli and nonno. I'd been too busy to call her before today, and she hadn't reached out either, so it sort of slipped my mind to update her. She didn't even offer to help with anything, and I certainly didn't ask. I didn't tell her about Vinny, either. I don't have the energy to hear her opinion.

After I hung up with her, I received picture updates from Lindsay, and the deli is coming along nicely. She said they needed an extra two days because the bathroom fixtures weren't going to be delivered on time. Typical. But now it allows me the weekend to relax and spend time with Vinny.

Dammit.

There I go again.

I can't help it, though. He's not the man I thought he was going to be.

I don't know why I thought going out with him would have led to immediate trouble and danger, but I was proven wrong, and I'm glad I was.

Vinny told me to let him know when I was finished with my work, but I can't wait until after class.

Me: I'm giving my oral report in class today and then I'll be free.

Vinny: Are you sure that's your only oral report for the day? Because I could've sworn you had another one tonight. I do too.

Me: You too? Were you good in school? Because I'm used to getting A's.

Vinny: Have they made a grading system yet where they give O's? Because then I'd be first in class, baby.

Me: Am I not in the running?

Vinny: We could be tied. I'll let you know after your orals tonight. My mouth is watering right now thinking about mine.

I shouldn't have texted him.

Now, all I can focus on is his mouth on me, and my panties dampen. I try to get back to organizing my flash cards, but I squirm in my desk chair, most definitely not focused on preparing for my exam anymore.

Me: You're distracting me. If I blank on my orals today because I'm thinking of your mouth on me and mine on you, then I'm going to be mad.

Vinny: You'll be amazing, *dolcezza*. But if you find yourself distracted, just know that if you don't ace it, I won't be touching you tonight and you won't be touching me. Got it?

Me: Yes, *bello*.

Vinny: Good girl. Now go study so I can reward you later.

Damn him.

I need to ace this exam today, because there's no way I'm going to be punished with a no touching rule when I've gone four days without any touching already.

CHAPTER 24
Vinny

I knock on Lexi's apartment door, and when she opens it, she's surprised to see it's me.

"What are you doing here?"

"Are you not happy to see me, *dolcezza*?"

"I am. I just…" She looks down at her sweatpants and tank top. "I didn't start getting ready to see you yet."

"I don't need you to dress up for me. You're beautiful." I grab her face for a long and slow kiss, savoring her taste after days of not having it. "I missed you, Lexi."

"I missed you, too," she admits, her soft spoken words making the days without her worth it. I want her to miss me. I want her to want to be with me.

I walk her inside and close and lock her door. "So, how did you do today?"

"I definitely aced it," she says, smiling against my lips.

I kiss her hard and walk her backwards until she hits the back of her couch. "Good. Time for my test." I turn her around and press at the spot between her shoulder blades. "Hold onto the couch, baby."

Lexi bends forward and grips the back ledge of her couch and I drop to my knees at her feet. I tug her sweatpants and panties down in one swipe and she gasps as I waste no time diving into the heaven between her legs.

"Vinny!" she cries out the moment my tongue slides through her wet folds.

I've been deprived of this sweet cream for too long to waste any time. I knew she'd be wet. I knew she'd be ready. I knew she'd be needy.

My girl is always needy.

Her legs start to give out and I wrap my arms around each leg to keep her upright while she gives me some of her weight on my face.

Fuck yeah.

I swirl my tongue around her entrance and slip it inside, groaning when she clenches around me.

Her legs shake in my grip, letting me know it won't be long before she's coming all over my tongue. She's been without too, and I can't have that.

I suck her tight little bud between my lips and Lexi cries out, giving me more of her weight as her arms struggle to hold her up.

Flicking my tongue over her clit until her entire body is shaking, I hold her up with one arm and shove two fingers inside her while sucking on her clit.

Lexi wails and collapses over the couch, but I keep going. I draw out her orgasm until her pussy stops pulsating around my fingers and I've licked her clean.

I kiss her pussy and then each of her ass cheeks, pulling her panties and sweats back up. I definitely earned my O, because my girl is so limp and spent, I have to lift her into my arms to lay her down on the couch.

I take the time to look around her living room, and a picture of her as a child with her mom and dad catches my eye. Her mom has blonde hair and blue eyes, and her dad is the classic Italian with dark brown hair and matching eyes. I was wondering how Lexi got her blue eyes.

Her family looks so happy in this moment that the photo was taken, and it makes me happy knowing she grew up with smiles and laughter.

There's another picture on her bookshelf of her as a little girl with her grandparents in front of the deli, and her grandfather is looking down at her with a massive smile while Lexi I grinning ear-to-ear at the camera.

"What are you looking at?" Lexi asks, propping herself up to look at me.

"Your pictures. You look so happy in them."

"I was."

"You're lucky. I don't think I have a single picture from my childhood with me smiling."

"Really? Why?"

"I know I had happy moments, but they weren't documented. Besides, when we each turned ten, it was time to step up and start our training."

"Training?"

"Yeah." I lift her feet and sit at the end of the couch, placing her legs over my lap. "We had responsibilities. Duties to the family that required us to be ready for whatever we might have to face when we took over. It was always in the plans that the second generation would take over for our parents, but it happened a lot sooner than we all anticipated."

"After your dad and uncle," she says softly.

"Yeah." I nod. "I hated my dad and uncles for putting us through what they did, always saying it was for the family and for our future. They said we'd never make it as Carfanos if we were weak. So, they made us resilient. I, of course, started combating all of it with girls and partying when I was fifteen, I think. I don't know, but I needed to release the tension I felt every minute I was at home or at my uncle's house. When they died, it was like a wakeup call, and I knew I needed to step up for Alec. I still party, but it's not like before."

"I'm sorry you didn't have the childhood you deserve."

"Didn't I?"

"No, Vinny." Lexi reaches for my arm and brings my hand to her lap, holding it in both of hers. "Everyone deserves to grow up in a house with loving parents and good memories that go beyond ten years old. We all don't get that, but that doesn't mean it's what we deserve. Did I deserve to have my dad taken away from me? I used to think if I was a better person, maybe he wouldn't have left me. But he didn't leave, and he wasn't gone as some sort of punishment to me. He had cancer. He was taken by a disease that knows nothing about who it's taking from. It just takes until there's nothing left. Then a few years later, I had my grandmother taken the same way. I didn't deserve that."

Tears are streaming down Lexi's cheeks, but her eyes are fierce and unwavering.

"You have the rest of your life to live, Vinny. Make it your own. And if you ever become a father, then you have the power to be different."

"Come here, baby." I pull her up by her arm and hold her to my chest. "I'm sorry. No, you didn't deserve that. I wish I was there to comfort you when you needed it."

"You are now," she murmurs against my neck.

I rub circles on her back and she tightens her arms around me. "And you're comforting me, *dolcezza,*" I whisper into her hair, closing my eyes and breathing her in.

CHAPTER 25

Lexi

My phone goes off for the second time and I pat around me on the bed to find it.

"Hello?" I answer groggily.

"Lexi? It's Lindsay," she says, a desperation in her voice that has my eyes flying open.

"What's wrong?"

"I'm so sorry. Something happened at the deli."

"What? Is my grandfather alright? Did he fall?"

"No, he's fine. But the work on the bathroom caused an unforeseen event to occur."

"Lindsay, what are you trying to say?"

"The toilet and sink were taken out because the new

ones were arriving today, but a pipe burst overnight, and the entire place is flooded."

"What?" I breathe, words failing me.

"I don't know what happened." She's panicking. "Everything's ruined. The new flooring, furniture, the refrigerated display cases, and I don't even know about the kitchen yet."

"Where's my grandfather?"

"He's here. When I arrived, he had already called the plumbers to get the water flow stopped."

"He didn't call me," I say throwing the covers off. "Why didn't he call me?"

"I don't know. I found out when I got here and knew I had to call you when I saw you weren't here."

"Thank you. I'll be there as fast as I can."

I throw my phone on the bed and quickly brush my teeth, wash my face, and get dressed in whatever I find first.

Vinny left early this morning to go to a meeting or something, and I fell back asleep. I didn't think I'd wake up to this.

When I pull up to the deli, I see Lindsay and nonno standing in the parking lot out back, and I run up to them, hugging my nonno.

"Why didn't you call me?"

"There was nothing you could do." He's defeated. I can see it in his eyes and in the slump of his shoulders.

"That's not the point." I go to look inside, by nonno grabs my arm to stop me.

"Don't." He shakes his head.

"Here, nonno, have a seat." I walk him over to a folding chair he keeps outside for breaks, and have him sit. "We'll figure this out. It's all going to be fine. I figured it out after the break-in, and I'll figure it out now. I'm going to call the insurance company to see where we go from here."

"Alright." He nods, rubbing his eyes.

I hate seeing him like this.

Pulling my phone out, I walk down the parking lot to make the call, and this one better go better than the last one.

CHAPTER 26

Lexi

Between $50,000 and $70,000.

Possibly upwards of $100,000.

That's how much it's going to cost for all the pipes to be replaced, to redo all the work we just did, and replace ruined equipment. And that's just the estimate.

I think I'm going to pass out.

Insurance, once again, isn't covering anything because plumbing isn't in my nonno's policy. I was going to go over the insurance policy when I got the chance after the improvements, but clearly the universe had the plan of piling shit on top of shit, and forcing me to find a way out of it for us.

Nonno is devastated. He thinks he should just sell the building as it is and get whatever he can from it to retire, but I'm not going to let that happen.

He can't give up.

First, the building won't sell for what he thinks it will. Second, what money is he going to live off of while waiting for the sale? Third, where would he live after selling the building? Fourth, what would he do in retirement?

His whole life has been the deli, and he's told me my entire life that he plans to work until he can't stand any longer. And even then, he still wants to run the place, only from one of the chairs at a table and not behind the counter.

He's old school, and seventy is too young for him to throw in the towel.

Which means I'm not throwing in the towel either.

Which also means I have to make a phone call I don't want to make, but will, for him. I'll just have to lie a little to get the information I need.

Pulling out my phone, I take a deep breath and tap Charles's name.

"Hey, Lexi, what's up?" he asks, the surprise in his voice evident. I never call him.

"Hi, Charles, I'm fine. I have a question for you, though."

"Sure, what is it?"

"I need to know if you know of any underground poker games in the city."

"Do you need money?"

"No, my friend does, and I told him you might know of

a place he can go where there'd be little to no questions and little to no rules."

"It's a male friend?"

"Yes," I lie. "Does that matter? He's a friend from school who needs money for his family and needs it quickly. I already told him asking me for suggestions is a path he can't un-walk down. He insisted."

"Good. You're a smart woman, Lexi. I only ask because the place I know of isn't for the faint of heart and isn't a place I'd feel comfortable recommending to a woman. There aren't many there."

And that's exactly why I'm lying to him.

I don't need him or my mom to worry, and I physically can't bring myself to ask, or take, his money. I don't see him wanting to help his wife's ex father-in-law, anyhow.

"That's considerate of you. But no, he's a him."

"It's in Chinatown. It used to be run by the Triads, but has since been taken over by the Bratva."

"The Russian mob?"

"The one and only. Are you sure your friend is desperate enough to go to a place like that?"

"I think so. He told me he doesn't care where he has to go or what he has to do."

"Alright, I'll send you the address. But, Lexi, warn him to be on his toes. I haven't been since it changed over, but a few friends have, and they say it's intense."

"I'll pass the message along. Thank you, Charles. I really appreciate this."

"You're welcome. You know, if you're ever in a situation

like your friend, you can come to me, right? I never want you to feel like you have to go to a place like that if you're in trouble. There are never any strings attached to my help, either. You know that, right?"

"I know. But thank you for saying it."

"Maybe when your mother and I get back from Chicago, we can have dinner?"

"That'd be nice." I didn't even know they were in Chicago.

"Good. Have a good weekend, Lexi."

"You too."

I hang up and take a moment to rethink my plan. But not for too long, because then I know I'll talk myself out of it.

I can handle myself.

I mean, how bad could it possibly be?

Vinny is in the mafia and he's a nice person. Granted, I only know he's nice to me, but still…

I don't have time to go to casino after casino to make the money.

Besides, if I'm able to win the amount I think I have the potential to win, then I can fix the deli and have enough left over to set my nonno up with a large savings for when he's ready to retire. If ever.

I know he'll ask me where I got the money, and I'll have to come up with a good stretch of the truth when the time comes. But right now, I'm more worried about what I'm going to tell Vinny about where I'm going tonight.

I think he'll know if I'm lying to him.

I have to, though.

I can't keep letting him help me like I'm a charity case he has to bail out simply because he likes me or wants a future with me.

I'm not a charity case. I can take care of myself and my family on my own.

What's that saying? Ask for forgiveness, not permission?

There's no way in hell I'd ever ask anyone for permission like I'm a child, but I can definitely think of a few ways to get Vinny to forgive me that will have him forgetting that he's mad at me for disappearing for a night to go to a Bratva gambling den.

If he ever finds out, that is.

CHAPTER 27
Vinny

Leaning back in my chair, I kick my feet up on my desk and dial Lexi. She picks up right away, which has me smiling.

"Hi, Vinny." I can hear her smiling, and my chest tightens, loving that she's happy that I called.

"Hi, *dolcezza*. What are we doing tonight? I miss you."

"You just saw me." Again, the smile in her voice is evident.

"That was this morning, Lexi. I need to see you soon. I need to kiss you. I need to hold you. Fuck it," I say, slapping my desk. "I need to be inside you. Your warm, wet pussy is the tight hug I need right now, *dolcezza*."

"Vinny," she says, her voice all breathy and turned on.

"See? I want to hear you say my name like that when I'm buried deep inside you and you're desperate to catch your breath."

"I…I can't tonight."

"Why not? Do you have plans with someone who can give you something better than multiple orgasms?"

"No, of course not. I'd much rather be the recipient of said orgasms, but Cassie and I are having a girl's night. I promised her days ago and she'll yell at me if I back out. She can be mean when she wants to be."

"I have no doubt. She seems like a firecracker."

"With that hair? Yeah, she is."

"Alright," I sigh. "I know I could convince you, but I'll save my real dirty talk for when you're here."

"Please do. Talk tomorrow?"

"I don't think I'll be able to wait that long. I'll need to hear your voice again." I sound like a desperate man and I don't give a fuck.

"You will?"

"Yeah, Lexi, I will. Why does that surprise you?"

There's a beat of silence before she answers. "Because it does. I'm not used to being missed or having someone want to talk to me just to hear my voice."

"I don't know how that's possible, *dolcezza*. You're the kind of girl that's missed. The kind that has men drinking until they pass out if they ever lose you. The kind that has a man knowing he'll be lost without you. The kind that has a man knowing he has to work every day to keep you because there's no shortage of others waiting in the wings to take his place if he fucks up. So, yeah, Lexi, I miss you and I want to hear your voice, and I want you to know it."

"Vinny." She breathes my name again and I hear her sniffle.

"Don't cry, baby. I didn't mean to make you cry."

"Then you shouldn't be so fucking nice."

I bark out a laugh. "Sorry about that. Want to come here and show me how much you hate when I'm nice?"

"I can't," she says solemnly, but there's a hint of something else in her voice. "I have to do that thing for my grandfather."

"I thought you were having a girl's night with Cassie."

"Oh, right. No, yes, I am. She's coming over and we're going to work on something for him."

Why is she lying to me?

Even without seeing her, I can tell she's lying.

"Is there anything I can do to help?"

"No, I'm good."

I want to push her on it, but I know pushing her will only lead to her backing away from me when all I want is for her to come closer.

I know she wants to be with me, but it still feels like she's holding back. Physically, she's with me 100% when we're together, and I fucking know it. There's no faking that. But emotionally...

Emotionally, she still has a few walls I have to climb before she's mine, and I'm going to climb them, no matter how long it takes. Fuck, I'll bust through them if I have to.

"Is something wrong, Lexi?"

"No," she says quickly, and I know she's still lying.

"You wouldn't tell me if there was, though, would you?"

"Why would you say that?"

"Just remember I'm here, okay? You just have to ask, and I'm there."

"I know," she whispers, regret seeping through the phone. Regret for what, I'm not sure, but she sounds like she's sorry for something she hasn't done yet.

"As long as you know." I rub the back of my neck. "I do have something to tell you, too, but it can wait until I see you."

"No, you can tell me now. Did something happen?"

"Ben finally gave the name of his partner. Eddie Fusillo. He's in the wind, though. He probably ran when he found out Ben was arrested."

"What does that mean? Are they not looking for him anymore?"

"There's a warrant out for his arrest. But no, there's no active manhunt."

Her silence speaks volumes.

"He's not a sophisticated criminal, Lexi. He'll be in custody soon."

"Alright," she says softly. "I have to go."

"I'll call you later."

"Okay," is all she says, hanging up.

She's disappointed. I hate disappointing her.

I have all our men on the lookout for Eddie, so I know he'll be in custody soon. But what's more pressing, is the fact that Lexi was lying to me about her plans tonight.

What could she be doing that she couldn't tell me?

I don't have time to dwell on it because my phone rings.

"Hey, Alec, what's up?"

"Are you bringing Lexi to dinner tonight? Tessa wants to know so she can make sure there's a place setting for her if she is."

"No, she's not." I rub my forehead. I forgot to even ask her.

"Did you ask her?"

"No, I didn't get the chance. But tonight is about you and Tessa, not me introducing Lexi to the family. Does Tessa need me to bring anything?"

"No. We've got it all covered. Just be at the house by six."

"See you then."

Tonight is our Sunday family dinner where all the extended family gathers at the Todt Hill house, but Alec and Tessa are using it as their announcement dinner as well.

Alec, Leo, and Luca all used our family dinners to introduce their women to the family, but they didn't all go so well. I want Lexi to know my family, but I don't want to give her a reason to distance herself from me if my mother doesn't give her a warm welcome.

The drive up to Staten Island is going to be a lonely one without my girl next to me.

I look at my empty passenger seat and pull my phone

out to send Lexi a text.

Me: Just thinking about you, *dolcezza*.

Lexi: What a coincidence. I was just thinking about you, too.

Me: Good. Keep thinking about me. Think about what I did to you last night and how much I can't wait to do it all over again.

Lexi: And you think about that thing I did on our first date. I never told you how much I liked when you told me what to do.

Fuck.

This wasn't a good idea.

I can't be hard up and thinking about Lexi choking on my cock when I have a two-hour drive, a family dinner, and a two-hour drive back before I can either beg Lexi to see me or beat one off in the shower, wishing she was on her knees and taking me deep in her hot mouth.

Me: Already there, baby. And if your goal was to have me hard, hot, and bothered, then you've accomplished that, my little tease.

Lexi: Good.

Me: And just for that, when I see you next, I want you on your knees with my cock down your throat before you even say hi.

Lexi: Yes, Vincenzo.

I groan, pressing the heel of my palm to my aching cock. She knows I love when she uses my full name.

Me: See you soon, Alexis.

I slip my phone back into the inner pocket of my suit jacket and drive out of the garage, needing the open road to get myself under control again.

Lexi has me so far gone for her, I can't even think straight anymore, and that's not good for a man in my position.

Being distracted 24/7 can cause mistakes to happen, and those mistakes can easily lead to someone, or our business, getting hurt.

The last thing I want is for anyone to get hurt because I'm not thinking straight. I have no problem living with Lexi on my mind 24/7. But when the inkling of her doubts, possible secrets and lies, and my own doubts of her not ready to commit to me and us are festering in the back of my head, I can't be who I need to be for everyone.

CHAPTER 28

Lexi

I'm fully aware this isn't the best idea. In fact, it's one of my most dumb and reckless ones, and yet here I am, driving into the city to go to a gambling den run by the Bratva. By myself.

The texts I exchanged with Vinny earlier didn't help, either. Guilt is making my stomach churn for lying to him, but I can't let it change my mission.

I'm doing this for my nonno, but I'm also doing it for me. I want to keep the deli alive and going even after my nonno is gone. Hopefully that won't be for quite a long while, but I'm not giving up on it. Ever.

The drive takes me just over two hours, and when I

reach the address Charles gave me, I see it's a Chinese restaurant, but the two large Russians standing outside smoking are a giveaway to what it really is.

I keep driving, needing to find a parking spot not too close, but still within a minute walking distance for an easy getaway later. Plus, I'm in heels and in a sketchy area of Chinatown that I'd much rather not be caught in later tonight dressed the way I am with undoubtedly the large amount of money I'll be carrying.

I round the corner to make a loop around the block, but someone is pulling away from the curb so I take their spot.

My heart is racing and my palms are sweating as I clutch the steering wheel.

I can do this.

I will do this.

I'm strong.

I'm more than capable.

Taking a deep breath, I close my eyes and see the image of nonno and Vinny in the newly renovated deli, laughing and speaking Italian to one another.

I take another deep breath and apply a fresh coat of deep red lipstick to my lips before turning my phone on silent and slipping both back into my small clutch purse.

Fluffing my hair, I climb out of my car and slide my hands down my sides to make sure I'm all covered. My outfit isn't one I'm used to wearing, but I knew I needed to give myself an extra leg up.

Being underestimated because of the way I look is always a plus. So is having the ability to distract the men at the table with a simple shift of my hair or my torso to accentuate my boobs.

It doesn't work on everyone, but I'm not exactly dealing with professionals here. At least, I'm more than certain I won't be.

I'm wearing a short skirt that's made of flat, silver, circular sequins, each one connected by a metal loop. There's a white fabric lining beneath so I'm not completely exposed, and I love the way it moves when I walk. I feel a little like a pop star ready to take the stage in it.

I've paired it with a semi-sheer white button-down shirt, and I've left the buttons undone down the center of my chest to show off the white lace corset bralette I have on beneath that can pass as another top. I've finished off the look with silver strappy heels and a silver clutch.

I feel like a lost party girl, which feeds into the persona I'm going for tonight. I'm a little rich Upper East Side college girl who's looking to gamble daddy's money as a way to get back at him for ignoring me and cheating on my mom with the maid.

Dramatic? Yes.

But I like a good backstory.

I get a few looks from those I pass as I walk down the block, and with each step, I slip a little deeper into the persona.

My nerves fade and my confidence skyrockets.

My face falls from any expressions I had to remain stoic and aloof, with a hint of prissy sass.

The two big Russian men just lit up fresh cigarettes, and

as I approach them, I look them up and down.

"Can we help you?" one asks, his accent thick.

"Yes, you can open the door for a lady, can't you?"

"Restaurant closed."

I flash them a smile. "I'm not here to eat, boys."

The one who hasn't spoken yet grins, flicking his ashes to the sidewalk. "We'll have to check for weapons."

I hold my arms out. "Does it look like I'm hiding anything?"

"It's the rules. Everyone is checked. Step inside."

I nod my agreement and he holds the door open for me.

"Hands out," one instructs, and I do as he says, making sure to keep my face neutral as he pats me down. His hands linger on my hips, and when he starts to go lower, I drop my arms and grip his wrist.

"I'm not up for exploration," I tell him, my voice level and forceful. His eyes meet mine and I hold his gaze, not backing down or looking away. "Understand?"

"*Da.*" Yes, he says. It's one of the only Russian words I know.

"I need to check your bag."

I open the clasp of my clutch and he pokes around, finding only my lipstick, compact mirror, phone, and a thick roll of cash. $10,000 to be exact.

He looks impressed. "You're here to play."

"I am."

He nods to his partner who opens the next door for me where there's another man waiting to guide me to where the games are.

The place is still set up like a Chinese restaurant, except only a few tables are occupied, and all of the men look to be Russian and there isn't any food in front of them. Just drinks, cigarettes, and their phones.

The men lift their eyes to me as I walk past them, and all I feel is death coming from them.

I shouldn't be here.

A cold chill runs down my spine, and I remind myself to keep my face free of any fear I'm feeling.

These men look like they'd kill me without batting an eye or having a morsel of regret.

I should've told someone, anyone, that I was coming here. If I could, I would send a quick text to Cassie to tell her that if she doesn't hear from me in three hours, to tell Vinny where I am.

Fuck, I should've told Vinny. But he would've stopped me. He would've just offered to give me the money rather than putting myself in this position. I couldn't do that. Correction, my pride couldn't do that.

We walk through the clean, no longer used kitchen, and when we reach what is supposed to be the walk-in refrigerator, he opens the metal door and there's nothing inside.

The door shuts behind me and that spike of fear lances down my spine again at being alone in a metal box where I know no one would hear me scream if I did.

He punches in a code on a keypad on the opposite side, and when the light flashes green, he opens another door to a room that's bustling with noise, clouds of cigarette and cigar smoke, and tables full of people gambling their money away.

CHAPTER 29
Vinny

"Hey, brother." Nico slaps my back and pulls me in for a quick hug. "How's everything?"

"Good."

"Where's Lexi tonight? You didn't bring her?"

"No, she said she's having a girl's night with Cassie."

"Sounds like you're skeptical about that."

"I am, but I didn't want to push. Have you talked to Cassie?"

"Why? You want to know if she mentioned what she's doing tonight to corroborate Lexi's story?"

"You're making her sound like a criminal."

"Sorry." He laughs. "Just relax, brother. Have a glass of

wine. Or something stronger." He pats my shoulder and then hugs our mother.

"Hey, ma."

"Hi, honey." She hugs Nico, but her eyes are on me. "Did I just hear you say something about a woman in Vincenzo's life?"

"Yes, you did. You have ears like a bat, don't you?"

"You know I do." She smiles. "How else do you think I would've found out all the stuff you two got up to growing up? So, what's her name? Who is she?"

I clear my throat and reach for the wine glass that's already poured on the table at one of the place settings. "Her name is Lexi. Alexis Manzato."

"An Italian girl?"

"Yes, ma. She's from AC and is in her senior year of college studying psychology and business."

"Will I get to meet her? You should have brought her tonight."

"Tonight is about Alec and Tessa, not me."

"What do you mean?"

Oh, shit.

I forgot no one else knows they're using tonight to make their announcement.

"Nothing. Just that I didn't want tonight to be about scrutinizing my girl."

"Your girl." My mom grins knowingly, pulling me in for a hug. "I'm happy for you, son," she whispers to me, giving me an extra squeeze.

"Thanks, ma."

"Alright everyone, time to eat," my aunt Anita announces.

I head into the kitchen to help bring out the dishes, and when we're all seated around the table, Alec clears his throat and stands. "This isn't just our usual Sunday dinner," he starts, looking down at Tessa who's smiling up at him. "We waited until everyone was together to tell you that Tessa's pregnant."

Bursts of excitement and echoes of congratulations ring out around the table.

"But there's more." Alec holds his hand out and Tessa takes it, standing at his side. "When we found out a month ago, we eloped."

"What?!" Anita yells. "You got married without your own mother? Without your family?"

"I'm sorry, ma, but I'm not putting any stress on Tessa or the baby just to have a ceremony that tells all of you what you already know."

"But we will be having a wedding," Tessa says, smacking Alec in the stomach with the back of her hand. "He already promised me one." She smiles, rubbing her stomach nonchalantly.

"Good. Because I want to see my son marry you," Anita says, taking her napkin and patting under her eyes. "I'm happy for you two." She stands and hugs them both first, and then everyone else around the table follows suit.

This dinner is a lively one, with the happiness of another union in the family. Leo and Abrianna's wedding is in a few months, and that, I know, is going to be a huge production.

The head of the Carfano family is getting married, and that will bring together every extended member of our family as well as the heads of the other three families – Melcciona, Capriglione, and Antonucci. It was four others, but there aren't any more Cicariellos to speak of to represent them.

Weddings are neutral ground. There's no business discussed or bad blood spilled. It's a day to show off your family and a day to show your power. And believe me, we're going to show a lot of power that day.

After dinner, the plates are cleared, more wine is poured, and dessert is served. In between, though, I excuse myself to the bathroom and check my phone to see if I have any texts or missed calls from Lexi, but there's nothing.

I press the call button by her name and it goes straight to voicemail. I try again, but still nothing.

Fuck.

I know I'm about to enter my crazy, possessive, and over protective mode, but I can't reel any of it back in. I can't shake the uneasiness in the pit of my stomach.

I send Nico a text to meet me in the hallway, and he shows up a few seconds later.

"Did you really just text me to meet you here?"

"Yes. Do you have Cassie's number?"

"Why?"

"Nico, I'm not messing around. Do you have it? I can't shake that something is wrong and I need to make sure Lexi is okay."

"Fine," he sighs, tapping on his phone screen and then turning it for me to see.

I quickly tap out her number and hold my phone to my ear, pacing the hall.

"Hello?" she answers.

"Cassie?"

"Who's asking?"

"Vinny. I got your number from Nico. Can I talk to Lexi? I have to ask her something and she's not answering her phone."

"Uhm, and you're calling me? She's not with me."

I stop pacing and look at Nico. "She's not?"

"No. Should she be? What's going on?"

"I don't know yet. I have to go." I hang up and squeeze my phone, wanting to throw it against the wall.

"She's not with her," Nico says, and I shake my head. "Maybe she's with her grandfather."

"She wouldn't need to lie about that. I need Stefano. Now."

Walking back into the dining room, everyone goes quiet when they see the look on my face. "Stef, I need you." I turn on my heel and stalk back down the hall to Michael's old office, and I can hear the footsteps of more than just Stefano following me.

"What the hell is going on, Vin?" Leo asks, closing the door behind him and all my cousins.

"I've been seeing someone and she lied to me today about her plans. Her friend just confirmed that. I need you to track her car and phone, Stef. I need to know where she is."

"Are you sure about this, Vin?"

"Yes," I hiss.

"Alright." He sits down at the desk and logs into the computer. "Give me her name and phone number." I rattle it off and he starts frantically typing away, then frowns. "Her phone isn't emitting a signal."

"I called her just a few minutes ago and it rang. It didn't go straight to voicemail like it was off."

"She could've been driving and then went somewhere with a blocked signal like a tunnel or parking garage." He keeps typing away. "I'm assuming you don't have her car's vin number on hand so I can get the GPS info, so I'll just…" he trails off, focusing on whatever he's doing. "Just give me a few minutes."

Those few minutes are tense, and when Stefano squints at the screen and curses, my stomach drops.

"What?"

"Her car is in Chinatown."

"What?" I bark, rounding the desk to look at the monitor myself. "What the fuck do you mean her car is in Chinatown? Where in Chinatown?"

Vinny zooms in. "South side. Around the corner from the Triads' old gambling house."

"Fuck," I curse, rubbing the back of my neck.

"The one the Bychkov's took over after we took out the Chen brothers?" Leo steps forward and asks.

"Yes," Stefano confirms, and my stomach sinks.

"Do you know that's where she is, though? Maybe

there's something else on the block," Leo offers as an option, but I shake my head.

"No, that's where she is. She fucking counts cards. She's good, too. She did it at The Aces last week to piss me off and get my attention."

"Oh, shit. That's impressive," my cousin Gabriel says, and I level him with a glare.

"But dangerous," Leo adds. "Especially where she is now."

Lexi is in a Bratva gambling den.

Alone.

And she lied to me about it.

"It makes sense that her phone isn't giving off a signal. They probably have signal jammers."

"I don't give a shit if it makes sense or not," I seethe. "She has no way of getting help if she needs it. I'm going to get her," I declare, but Leo puts his hand out to stop me from leaving.

"You can't just rush in there and get her out, Vin."

"Why the fuck not?"

"Because it's Bychkov territory."

"Since when has that mattered? Do you think I won't do whatever I need to to ensure her safety?"

"No one's questioning that, but I'm not letting you go there how you are right now and causing trouble. You said she's good, and she clearly knows what she's doing if she knew where to go and walked in there willingly."

"Leo," I warn, and he fists my shirt.

"I'm not saying we're not going there to make sure she

makes it out okay. I'm saying we're not storming in there like she's been kidnapped. If she doesn't walk out of there by midnight, then we'll go in and get her. Okay?"

"Eleven," I correct, and he nods.

"Fine. Eleven."

"It's already ten o'clock, and it'll be at least a forty-minute drive, so you better go now," Stefano says. "I'll stay here and monitor her signal to keep you updated."

I walk out of the office and back down the hall where the rest of my family looks at me expectantly.

"Sorry, but something came up and we have to go."

"Is it Lexi? Is she okay?" my mom asks.

"I don't know. That's why I have to go."

"Alright, honey." She gives me a quick hug, worry etched on her face.

"Sorry to ruin your night, *sorellina*." I pull Tessa in for a hug, careful not to squish her still flat stomach where my niece or nephew is growing.

"Don't worry about it. I have chocolate cake, so I can't be upset," she assures me. "Go make sure Lexi is okay."

I give everyone else a wave of my hand and storm out of there, needing to get to my girl.

"Jesus, Vin, wait for us!" Leo calls after me when I'm halfway out the door.

CHAPTER 30
Lexi

My poker is a little rusty, but I've been holding my own. And aside from the fact that I feel like one of the guys along the wall watching the room is going to pull his gun out at any moment and shoot me or anyone else here, I've managed to focus and pick up the tells of those at my table after a few hands.

My own poker face consists of many rolled in one. I like to give false ones at first to lure the other players into thinking they know what hand I have. Like, if I have a bad hand, I scratch my chin, and if I have a good hand, I tap the table. Then I'll scratch my chin when I have a winning hand and bet it all, making the table think it's a sure thing they'll win. But I win, and I keep winning, much to the displeasure of the others at my table.

"You seem to know how to win," someone says to the right of me in a thick Russian accent. I look up to see who it belongs to, and it's a man who looks to be in his mid to late thirties and has been in a fight or two. Or fifty. And the hard, lifeless stare tells me he's won every single one of them.

I can tell he's not a man who will be impressed with flirting, so I go with confidence. "I do."

"It looks like you need more of a challenge."

"I think I'm doing just fine taking their money."

"*Da*. But you can take more money from richer men."

"That's an intriguing offer."

"Come." He waves another man over who collects my chips, giving me no other choice but to follow him.

I'm sandwiched between them and feel the eyes of many flit to me as I walk through the tables. They're all probably thinking what I am. It's a walk of death. Or a walk where I'm taken and used as they see fit.

Once again, I really should have told someone I was coming here. If I get sold into a sex trafficking ring, no one will know where to start looking for me. Vinny would look, I know he would, but he wouldn't know where to start.

I'm led to a hallway blocked off by another big scary Russian who steps aside to let us through.

I can't back out now.

I can't show fear.

There's only one way out of this, and that's walking down this nondescript hallway with two Russian mobsters who could overtake me in a second.

I'd fight. I'd fight tooth and nail if it meant I got to see Vinny again and apologize for lying about what I was doing tonight. I'm never going to be this stupid again.

I want to feel his arms around me.

I want to feel my heart flutter when he kisses me and my skin flush when he touches me.

I want to hear him call me *dolcezza* when he's deep inside of me and tell me how much he loves being inside of me.

I'm picturing Vinny's sexy little smirk as we turn a corner in this creepy hallway, and I breathe a silent sigh of relief when I see another muscled man guarding the entrance to another room. This one only has two occupied tables in it, with five men at one and two women and four men at the other.

"You sit at that one." My guide points at the table of five men.

"Have to make sure there's at least one woman at each table to keep the men honest, huh?"

"Not necessarily," he clips.

"I don't mind." I walk over to the table with the man carrying my chips in tow, keeping my confidence game up.

The men at the table look me up and down, and I give them all a smile where I simply curl my lips up, but it doesn't reach my eyes.

I'm dealt in, and with these guys, it takes everything I know to keep up. They're better at hiding their tells than the amateurs in the other room.

A small tick of their jaw, a tap of their straw in their

drink, a nose wrinkle, eye twitch, and a blank stare. I get them all and I use them all.

Their frustrations when I keep winning becomes more evident as the night progresses, and the tension is making me think of ways to quietly quit while I'm ahead.

I can guess what each of these men do based on how they bet and take risks. The two guys in three-piece suits are probably commodities traders who need to keep the rush going after work hours.

The one in black jeans, a white t-shirt, and an expensive leather jacket gives me the vibes of a trust fund baby who's dwindling his inheritance down one hand at a time.

The one drinking whiskey, with his suit jacket draped on the back of his chair and the sleeves of his white button down rolled up to his elbows, is definitely a CEO or COO who makes more money than he knows what do with, so he bets it away without a care, knowing he'll make it back the next day or week.

Then there's the guy across from me. He's just a regular guy who's in over his head. He's the guy that thinks he's a good poker player, but luck hasn't been on his side for some time. He still comes here, though, hoping it will.

I can tell he thinks he has a winning hand, but when I lay my cards on the table, his face falls and then turns red.

"How the fuck?" he growls, spitting anger. "You–" he cuts himself off. "Who the fuck let you in here?"

"Calm down, man," CEO says, sipping his whiskey. He tips his glass to me with a smirk like Vinny, but it doesn't have the same effect on me. "She won. Get over it. Maybe you're the one who shouldn't be let in here anymore. I can't imagine you have much left to gamble with."

"You fucking bastard!" Regular guy pushes up from his chair and leans forward on the table like he's going to either fight someone or steal the chips he's lost.

"Time to leave." The bodyguard from the door appears behind him and places his hand on his shoulder.

"Don't fucking touch me!" he yells, spinning around and winding his arm back like he's going to punch the big Russian wall of muscle, but the Russian easily captures his fist and twists his arm around his back.

"AH!" regular guy yelps, his face twisting in pain. "Get off me!"

"You're done here. We warned you last time. Now you know what happens." His Russian accent makes everything he says that much more intimidating, and I keep my face neutral as the guy is led out of the room, the pain on his face morphing into pure fear.

The atmosphere in the room shifts, and I want to get the fuck out of here, but I can't be the first to walk away after that.

"He doesn't like losing to a woman," CEO says to me, that smirk still in place. He's undoubtedly good-looking, but nowhere near as handsome as Vinny.

"Some men aren't man enough to lose to a woman, I suppose. You don't seem to mind, though, do you?" I say back, and his smirk turns into a full-blown cocky grin.

"No, sweetheart, I don't mind. I have plenty to lose to you, too, in case you were worried about me."

"I wasn't." The day traders laugh and the trust fund baby breaks his emotionless mask by tipping one side of his mouth up.

"After that, though, I think I'm going to call it a night. Maybe you can take more of my money some other time, gorgeous," day trader one says to me, with the second nodding his agreement.

They both get up and leave, taking what little chips they have left with them to cash out.

"Are you gentlemen going to call it a night, too, or do you have more to lose?"

A gunshot goes off somewhere nearby and I jump, my heart rate going from rapid to damn near heart attack status.

Did they just kill him?

Did I just get a man killed?

I take slow breaths to keep my calm exterior in check despite how much I'm freaking out on the inside, and look around to see the reactions of those still in the room. Not everyone is as good at hiding their emotions, and when everyone stands, I realize there's some unspoken rule of gunplay ending the night. Fine with me.

"Cash out and leave," one of the guards standing around the room bellows.

The dealer hands me a bag from under the table and I scoop all my chips into it, making sure to give her a few as a tip.

I won way more than I need. Like, way more. But I can think about what I'm going to do with it all when I'm safely out of here and on my way back home.

I follow the other players to a different back room further into the building where there are stacks of cash on a table surrounded by five armed men.

Jesus.

I'm in way over my head.

I wait patiently in line, making sure I'm not the last one, and press myself against the wall to keep upright. These heels are pinching my pinky toes and my legs aren't feeling as reliable as I'd like right now.

Player after player toss their bags of chips on the table where two men count it separately and then a third hands them their cash. Minus the house's fee of course.

When it's finally my turn, I heave my bag of chips onto the table and the men look at me for a beat longer than they did anyone else.

I stand there and wait as they take ten to fifteen minutes each to count the chips out. One writes the amount on a piece of paper and slides it to the cash guy who walks over to the corner of the room to grab a metal briefcase.

I guess I should be flattered that I've earned a briefcase and not just a few sacks to carry out.

The air in the room shifts, and the hairs on the back of my neck tickle, letting me know someone important just walked into the room. The men who were counting my chips bow their heads in respect and I turn to face the man who warrants such respect.

"You've never been here before. I would have remembered."

"You're correct," I say simply, surprised when my voice

comes out steady.

"You come here and we have an incident. Coincidence, or no?"

"Yes, it is. I didn't know him and he seemed to have a problem with losing."

"He's been dealt with. As for you," he says, stepping closer, his cold eyes assessing me. "You should find somewhere else to play. You're bad for business."

"You won't see me again."

"We're taking an extra fee for our trouble tonight," he tells me, and the guy placing my money in the briefcase doesn't add the last ten stacks of money to it.

So, the fee for causing trouble is a hundred grand?

I'm not about to argue though, if it means I get to walk out of here unscathed.

"Sounds fair."

"More than fair." The briefcase is closed and locked, and handed to the man in charge. "I'll walk you out."

I'm escorted back the way I thought I might never walk again, and I'm so close to breathing a breath of fresh, free air, that I also thought I might never have again.

We reach the main room that's still being cleared out, and it's as if everyone knows not to look our way.

I've been in fight or flight mode for hours now, and keeping up appearances has been slowly draining me.

I need air. I need to scream. I need to cry. I need to…I don't know. I just need to get out of here and make sure no one follows me back home.

"Remember what I said," he tells me, handing me my

briefcase by the door.

"I will."

The heavy metal door is opened for me and I walk out into the frigid city air, not even feeling it at this point after everything. It doesn't even touch me.

"You fucking bitch!" Regular guy emerges from the shadows of a nearby dumpster and I freeze. I'm glad they didn't kill him, but I do see dried blood around his nose and mouth, as well as a bruise forming around his eye. But it's the limp as he slowly approaches me that has me seeing the blood stain blooming on his jeans.

They shot him in the leg. And then what? Threw him out the door?

"You need a doctor," I tell him, taking a step backwards.

"What I need is my money back."

"What you need is to stop where you are." I hold my hand up. "Or do you want me to go knock on the door and tell them you're still here?"

Where the hell did those two scary bodyguards go that were outside before?

His face thunders as he takes another hobbled step towards me. "I want my money."

The door I came out of opens to let two more men out, and every cell in my body is screaming at me to run. To just run and hope I make it to my car before my money is stolen, I'm attacked, or worse.

I just need to get out of here.

I take another step backwards, but keep my eyes on the threat. If I had to, I know I could outrun him in his state, even with my heels. But my car is still around the block and I'd have to be very careful not to twist my ankle or break a heel.

My eyes are on regular guy as he takes another few steps towards me when a car pulls up and screeches to a halt at the curb.

"Lexi." My name is spoken in a low and angry growl, and my shoulders relax on my next exhale.

Vinny.

I take my eyes off the man who continues to approach me, my sole focus on my man coming to my rescue just when I need him.

Vinny's eyes are on me, covering every inch of me in a matter of seconds to make sure I'm okay. When he's satisfied, he turns his gaze to the man approaching me. "If you take one more fucking step towards her, I'll put another bullet in you, and it won't be in your goddamn leg."

"She stole from me."

"I don't give a fuck. If you don't get the fuck out of here, I'm going to finish what they started. You get one chance to make the right choice."

"Do we have a problem out here?" The same man who walked me out asks in his thick Russian accent.

"No. Just picking up my girl," Vinny replies in a cool tone despite the anger I see simmering in him.

"You send her in here to cause trouble, Carfano?"

They know each other?

"Is that what she did?" Vinny raises his eyebrows in feigned surprise. "She won't be back. I can assure you of that."

"She already knows she's not welcome back. *Ponimaî?*"

"Understood." Vinny places his hand on my lower back and my body momentarily relaxes before tensing again when I feel his anger flowing through me.

"Get in the car, Alexis," he says in my ear so only I can hear.

CHAPTER 31
Vinny

I open the passenger door for Lexi and she gets in without looking at me and without saying a word.

I'm fucking fuming, and it takes a lot to get me this angry.

I walk around the car to my door, making sure I keep an eye on the Russians. I took off from the house a minute before my brother and cousins, so now their SUVs pull up and I raise my chin and tilt my head to my car to tell them I have her.

I don't linger. I don't want to be around the Bychkovs any more than I need to be. Their branch of the bratva took over the southside of Chinatown's gambling operations after we took out the Chen brothers a year and a half ago. While the Triads were fighting over who was next in line, the Bychkovs were able to step in and take over part of their business with little resistance

I peel away from the curb and look in my rearview mirror to see the three black SUVs following me. One makes the first turn to get Lexi's car, and after a few blocks with the others still behind me, I peel away from them and weave in and out of traffic, needing to get out of the city as fast as I can.

Neither of us says anything as the minutes stretch on. I drive like I'm in the fucking Indy 500, and she clutches her briefcase of money. It looks a lot like the one I put her money in when she hustled me.

"My car," she says quietly, but in the thick, tense air, it's deafening. "I drove here."

"Someone's got it."

"How?"

"My cousin can hack anything, remember? But that's not what we need to talk about."

My hands tighten on the steering wheel when she falls silent again.

"You're mad."

"That's stating the fucking obvious, Lexi."

"Don't speak to me like that," she says fiercely.

"In this instance, I will. Do you even know who runs those games? Do you know how lucky you are to have walked out of there? That I showed up when I did? Why were you even there?"

"How did you find me?" she asks instead of answering any of my questions.

"There's no hiding in my world. If I want to find you, I can, and I will. I knew you were lying about what you were doing tonight, and when you didn't answer any of my calls or texts, I called Cassie and she confirmed you two weren't together. And as I said, my cousin can hack anything. Stefano located your car, and when he said it was around the corner from that restaurant, I swear I almost had a fucking heart attack. Why did you lie to me? Why were you there?"

"I needed money."

"Why?"

"For the deli."

"You had money for the deli. You fixed it."

"A pipe burst overnight and the whole place flooded. Now all the pipes in the entire building need to be replaced, we need to redo all the updates we just did, and I need to replace the savings lost in the robbery."

"You couldn't find the time to mention it today? We talked. We texted. Why didn't you tell me?"

"Because it's my responsibility. I can take care of it myself."

"And you didn't want my help." It's not a question. It's a statement. She's so damn stubborn that she chose to put herself in danger in order to avoid asking me for help.

"No, I didn't want your money. There's a difference."

"So, you decided it was better to go into a Bratva run gambling den? Do you understand how dangerous that was? They had signal jammers so I couldn't call or text you and you couldn't call for help if you needed it. How did you even know about it?"

"My mom's husband."

"He has connections to the Russians?"

"What? No, he's a wealthy businessman who used to gamble a lot. Why are you so mad?"

"Because anything could have happened to you!" I shout, tightening my grip on the wheel again, my knuckles turning white. "Starting with that fucker who was about to rob you, and ending with every imaginable scenario those fucking men in there could think of doing with you and to you. Do you understand that? Do you get that if I didn't show up…" I grind my teeth.

"I would've been fine," she says confidently, really believing that.

"You think so?" I scoff.

"You doubt me. I'm not a helpless little girl who needs the big bad mafia man to swoop in and save her at every turn. I've taken care of myself just fine for most of my life."

"You don't need anyone, is that it? You want to do everything yourself? You want to spend the rest of your life never letting anyone in? What the fuck are we even doing, Lexi?"

"What do you mean?"

"I mean what I said. What are we doing? You clearly think you don't need me, or anyone, for anything."

"Because I don't want money from you, that means I don't want or need you?"

"Fucking Christ, it's not about money, Lexi."

I feel her eyes on me, studying me, and when we reach a red light, her soft voice rings out, "I need you."

I look at her, her face lit by the glow of the city lights coming through my heavily tinted windows.

Those three words.

Those three damn words are powerful coming from her.

"I need you, Vinny. The moment I walked in there, I wish I would've told you where I was. The thought of you and us and seeing you again was what drove me to stay calm and do what I went there to do so I could come home to you. And when you pulled up back there and I heard your voice, I've never felt relief like that. I didn't tell you because I knew you'd offer to help, and I don't want your money. I don't want to be some financial burden you feel you have to help just because we're... Because I'm..."

"Together? Mine?" I finish for her, and she nods.

A horn blares behind us and I speed off to the next red light.

"If you can't even admit or say it out loud, then your sentiments don't mean much, do they? Because I've thought of you as mine since I asked you to dance with me in the club."

"You have?"

"You know I have," I tell her, my words slicing through the air. "I called you my damn wife before I even knew your name."

"I know," she agrees softly.

Lexi puts her hand palm-up between us and I engulf her smaller one in mine, entwining our fingers. I bring our joined hands to my lips and kiss her knuckles.

"There's been no one else since I laid eyes on you, *dolcezza*. You're the missing piece to my puzzle. A perfect fit, made just for me. I know if you were to walk away, you'd take more than just a piece of me with you. You'd leave me with a gaping void I'd never be able to fill again, and you don't seem to get that. You don't seem to get that I'd do anything for you. I'd do anything to protect you. I'd give you anything you need, want, or desire. No matter how big or small, if it made you happy and made you smile, then I would do it."

I hear her sniffle and I look over to see her swipe her cheeks. "Pull over."

My heart twists. "*Dolcezza*."

"Can you please pull over?"

"I'm not letting you out alone at night in the city."

"I don't want to get out. Just pull over."

I park in the next empty street spot I see and look at Lexi, her blue eyes shining from tears.

She reaches up and cups my cheek, and I lean into her touch.

"I'm sorry," she says, regret dripping from those words and ringing clear in my ears. "I didn't mean to scare you, or upset you, or make you doubt me and how I feel about you. I need you too, Vinny. I've been fighting that fact and denying it when it's been there the entire time. It's you. You didn't hesitate to give up your night to help me when you didn't even know me, and you've kept being there even when I yelled at you and told you to leave me alone. I can't tell you how happy I am that you didn't listen."

She blinks out more tears, and this time I wipe them away.

"You're mine just as much as I'm yours," she continues, and the admission has my heart soaring. "I'm sorry I lied about tonight and put myself in a position to make you worry. I knew if I told you, then you would tell me not to do it, and I would've listened." She shakes her head, pleading with her eyes to get me to understand her.

"I know I messed up tonight. I know I shouldn't have been there. I lied to Charles to get him to tell me about any games he knew about, and once I walked in there, I knew it would look bad if I just turned around and asked to leave. So I pushed my fears aside and did what I do best. Win. But then it all took a turn when that guy lost all his money and started yelling at me. He was hauled away, beaten up, and shot. I thought they killed him, Vinny. I thought I was responsible for a man's death until he came out of the shadows and started yelling at me again. I thought I was going to have to run for my life to my car, and then I heard your voice, and I've never been more relieved in my life. Thank you."

"Anytime, *dolcezza*. If you need me, I'm there."

"Thank you," she whispers.

"I love you, Lexi. So fucking much." I cover her hand on my cheek with my own and turn my face to kiss the center of her palm. "I know you can do any and everything on your own, but you don't need to anymore. I want you to share your life with me. The good, bad, and everything in between."

"I want that too."

"No more secrets?"

"No more secrets," she agrees.

Lexi lets the metal briefcase slide to her feet and she tucks her leg under her, using it as leverage to lift herself closer to me.

Pressing her forehead to mine, she cups my face with both hands and pauses, her lips an inch from mine.

Even if she can't say it back right now, I know she loves me. I can feel it. I can feel it right now as if she's telling me silently with her mind and hoping I can hear her.

"I hear you, *dolcezza*," I whisper against her lips, and she gasps – a sharp intake of breath that brings my lips closer to hers.

Lexi slides her hands to the back of my head and finally closes the last sliver of space between us.

She kisses me like she's telling me she loves me too, and I'm momentarily stunned by the flood of emotions swirling around me like a damn whirlpool – pulling me towards the center and taking me down a rabbit hole where I don't know where, or if, I'll land safely. But if I have Lexi with me, then I welcome the ride.

My life was never one with a guaranteed safe landing, so why would it be that way when I fall in love?

I kiss her back with everything I'm feeling, and feel the moment she decides to free fall with me. It's the moment I've been waiting for since the beginning.

I grip the side of her neck possessively and tip her chin

up with my thumb, angling her exactly how I want her so I have all the access to her that I want.

Her lips part on a moan and my tongue delves inside her mouth, tangling with hers and making me see fucking stars.

"Vinny," she moans, tearing her lips away and gasping for air.

"Yes, *dolcezza*?"

"I need you," she says desperately.

"You have me, baby."

Lexi scratches the back of my head, digging her nails into my scalp. "I need you to fuck me. Now. I'm feeling too much and I need you to take it. I need to give it to you so you know. Please," she begs, and there's no way I'd ever deny my girl anything she wants. Especially this.

"Sit back, baby." I wait for her to be situated back into a seated position before I peel away from the curb and speed off down the block.

I can feel her practically vibrating in her seat, and when we reach the Lincoln Tunnel, I don't wait any longer.

"Take your panties off," I instruct, and she doesn't even hesitate. I love my girl when she's needy. "Let me have them." She dangles them from her fingers between us and I snatch them, bringing them to my nose to inhale her sweet scent. "Mmm," I hum, then suck on the wet spot her sweet cream has already created. "I can't get my mouth on you until we get home, but I won't make you wait, *dolcezza*."

She lets out a strangled little moan and I loop her lace thong around the gear shift.

"I like this outfit," I rasp, tracing my finger up her bare

thigh. "But I don't like knowing every man in there saw you like this."

"They looked, but only you can touch."

"You've got that right, baby." I grip her thigh and squeeze her heated flesh. "Turn towards me and give me your left leg." I drape her long leg over my lap and caress her soft skin, reminding myself over and over to keep focus on the road ahead of me, too. "Lift your skirt. Let me see that pretty pussy I can't wait to be inside when we get home."

Lexi gives me a seductive little smile and takes the short hem of her skirt and raises it to her hips. She leans against the door and presses her leg into me, tilting her hips up to give me a view I'll never forget.

"*Così fottutamente bella.*"

She's so fucking beautiful.

"Touch yourself, *dolcezza.*"

"I want *you* to," she says, dragging her hands up her inner thighs.

I encircle my fingers around her delicate ankle. "I want to watch you."

"You should be watching the road."

"I can multitask. And if you do this for me…" I run my hand up to her knee and back down to her ankle. "Then I'll give you what you want. You start, and I'll finish." I lick my lips, eager for a taste.

"Promise?" she coos, running a finger through her pussy. She holds it up for me to see it glistening with her juices. "I'll let you have a taste if you promise your fingers are the ones buried in me when I come, and not mine."

"Oh, I promise, *dolcezza*." Grabbing her wrist, I bring her hand to my lips and suck her sweetness from her finger.

"Then watch away, *bello*."

I bite her finger and she moans, my already hard cock now painfully straining against the fabric of my pants. "You think I'm handsome, *dolcezza*?" Hearing her call me *bello* makes my fucking chest swell with confidence. I've been told I'm good-looking many times, by many women, but hearing it from Lexi is the only time it's ever mattered.

What she thinks of me is the only opinion that matters.

"Yes," she sighs, and I swirl my tongue around her finger, giving her a preview of what I'm going to do with my tongue on her pussy later.

Lexi takes one of her delicate fingers that I'm well aware has the capability to both bring me closer with a mere crook and bring me to my knees with a point downward, and circles her clit.

She moans, and I bite down on her finger again. "I love that sound. Keep going, *dolcezza*."

My eyes dart between the road and my girl, and as her scent of arousal fills my car, I find my foot pressing down harder on the gas pedal.

Lexi spreads herself as wide as my car will allow and keeps her eyes on me while she plays with her pussy.

I let go of her hand and it falls to her thigh. Her chest rises and falls in quick breaths and her eyes grow heavy with the weight of her desire.

"*Bello*," she whispers, and I smile, scraping my teeth over my bottom lip.

"That's it, baby. Keep showing me how much you wish it were my fingers." Lexi circles her clit and then plunges two fingers inside her pussy. "Good girl," I praise, caressing her calf.

"Vinny, I…" She gasps, closing her eyes.

I slowly slide my hand up to her knee, but then stop halfway up her thigh. "You ready for me?"

"Yes. You promised."

"And I keep my promises. But first, I want you to take that hand you've been fucking yourself with and taste your sweetness. Taste what I do to you."

With a ghost of a smile on her lips, Lexi brings her coated fingers to her mouth and paints her lips like she's applying lip gloss.

Fuck me.

I wish I could kiss her right now.

The tip of her little pink tongue peeks out and rims her lips, capturing her essence. "Mmm," she moans, and I slide my hand closer to her heaven. So close now, I feel her heat radiating out of her.

"You promised," she reminds me, needing me.

"I know." I smile over at her and glide my fingers along the crease juncture of her thigh and pussy, making Lexi purr like a little cat and tilt her hips towards me. "So eager. What did I promise you again?" I tease, and she grunts, frustrated. "Oh, right…this." I plunge two fingers inside her wet, hot center, and we both groan. "Fuck," I grunt. "Lexi, baby, *dolcezza*. You're fucking perfect."

From this angle, I can't rub her clit like she needs, and

she quickly realizes the same thing, taking matters into her own hands and doing it herself.

I work my fingers in and out of her – spreading, twisting, and curling them.

Lexi chokes out a moan, pressing her leg that's on my lap against my cock.

She's so fucking wet. Her pussy is leaking and making a sexy sloshing sound every time I penetrate her. I take her cum that's dripping down her ass and let it coat my thumb before I press at her tight ring of muscles back there.

"Ohmygod," she says in a rush. "Vinny, what are you doing?"

"Fulfilling my promise."

With a little more pressure, my thumb slips into her, and at the same time, I add a third finger inside her pussy, stretching her so she can feel me filling her. I want her burning in the same fire I am watching the pure fucking pained bliss painted all over her features as she detonates.

Her inner muscles clamp down on my fingers, squeezing them together in my own form of blissful pain.

I slowly pump my thumb in her ass, drawing out her orgasm.

Her pussy pulses, her sweet cream flooding my hand and seat beneath her.

"That's it, *dolcezza*. Mark your territory with your cum. No one sits here but you from now on, so give me more, *bella*."

I shove my thumb all the way inside her ass and my fingers all the way to my knuckles in her pussy while using my pinky to press her finger harder against her clit.

"Vinny!" she shouts, and I inadvertently press down on the gas pedal as she explodes for a second time, melting into her seat.

I wasn't kidding when I said it's hers now. It is. No one else will ever fucking sit there but her. Her whole essence is infused in my car now, making it ours, not just mine.

Lexi's eyes roll back and she collapses against the door – spent and exhausted like a beautiful goddess.

I gently remove my hand and lick my fingers clean.

We still have a while before we're home, so I take one last long look at her pretty pussy and then maneuver her leg back to her side of the car.

Pushing her hair away from her face, I see she's already passed out, and I smile, loving that she'll wake up and still feel the result of what just happened between her legs.

She scared me tonight.

I don't know what I would've done if something happened to her. That's not true. I know exactly what I would've done. Either stormed in there and shot the place up, or had Dante, our family's hitter, rig up some explosives and blown the place to fucking smithereens. Consequences be damned.

Lexi is mine.

Mine to protect. Mine to care for. Mine to love.

She's my girl, and now that I have her, I won't let anything happen to her.

I've been playing with a missing card from my deck my entire life. And while everyone else seems to get dealt the good hands, I'm always left one card short from winning it all.

She's the wild ace that's been eluding me, but now that I have her in my grasp, I'm the luckiest bastard in the fucking world.

With her, it's a royal flush every day.

With her, I'll always have the best hand in the game.

CHAPTER 32

Lexi

"Wake up, *dolcezza.*"

"No," I mumble, and Vinny chuckles.

"We're home."

"Home?"

"Yeah, baby. Home."

"What's in it for me if I wake up?"

"Orgasms. As many as you want."

"Three," I say without thought.

"Only three?"

"Mhmm."

"Alright, let's go. Unless you want me to carry you?"

"I can walk." I yawn and stretch my legs out.

Vinny gets out and rounds the car to open my door. I grab the briefcase at my feet and take his hand to help me out. My skirt falls back into place and I feel the slickness between my legs, making my cheeks heat as I look back at the seat.

"That's your seat, *dolcezza*. Now, every time you're in it, I'll have to make you come." He winks, and my cheeks heat further. "You can't get shy on me now, Lexi. I have so much more I want to do with you."

"You can start now if we hurry upstairs," I suggest, and he gives me my favorite smile.

"How much did you win tonight?" he asks, eyeing my case.

I roll my lips between my teeth. "300."

"You're carrying 300 grand in your hand right now?"

"Yes. It would've been 500, but there were some extra fees added on for causing trouble."

"Despite the circumstances, that's so fucking sexy, baby."

"You want to see?" I ask playfully, biting my lip and winking.

"Upstairs." He winks back, and my heart swells with love for him. I don't know why I couldn't say it before, but he knew. The words got stuck in my throat and I couldn't say anything. But he knew. He felt what I was trying to say, and it was the greatest gift he could give me. Understanding and patience.

He understands me. He knows me. *He loves me.*

He takes the case from my hand and we somehow make

it upstairs without stopping to tear each other's clothes off. But the second he closes his apartment door, I push away from him and back up towards his room, unbuttoning my top as I go. I drop it in the hall and I reach for the ribbon at my back that's keeping my lace bralette together. I tug it loose and hold the fabric to my chest, waiting until I have the whole thing free before pulling it from my chest.

Vinny's hands flex at his sides and his eyes flare with heat when I slide my hands up my hips to cup my breasts, continuing to walk backwards towards his room.

He starts to take longer strides towards me, and when I know I'm close to his room, I turn around and unzip my skirt, shimmying my hips until it falls to my feet.

I smile and wink at him over my shoulder, and when I step out of my skirt, Vinny cages me in against the wall.

"You owe me what you promised in our texts earlier, *dolcezza*."

His hand skirts up my thigh and hip, and I have to focus to remember what I promised.

What did I…

Oh, right.

Smiling, I spin to face him and grab his jacket, pulling him into his room. Like he wanted, I don't say anything. I push his jacket from his shoulders and get to work on quickly unbuttoning his shirt. I push that from his shoulders too, and run my hands down his chest, smiling when his stomach muscles flex under my touch.

The bulge of his cock needing to be free has me biting my lip. I kneel at his feet and make quick work of his pants.

Tugging them down to his ankles, I waste no time pushing Vinny to the bed and taking him in my mouth.

"Fuuckk," he groans, bringing his hand to the back of my head.

I take him all the way to the back of my throat and he grunts, fisting my hair.

"That's it, baby, take me deep into that hot mouth of yours." I moan around him and he pulls me back off him until my lips are wrapped around just the tip. My eyes meet his. "I love seeing you like this, *dolcezza*." He tweaks one of my nipples and I moan around the head of his cock, causing him to shove me just a little more down his length. "You like have my cock in your mouth, don't you?" he asks, and I nod. "I know."

Vinny pushes me down his cock until he hits the back of my throat, then pinches my nipple when I do, making me moan.

"Again," he demands, pinching my nipple again so I'll moan around him. "Fuck yes, baby." His voice is rough and raw with need.

I grip him at his base and squeeze him upwards, meeting where my mouth stops.

I take back control, but after a minute, he pulls me off him, hooks his hands under my armpits, and lifts me up. Spinning me around, Vinny tosses me on the bed and he's on top of me before I even know what's happening.

"You didn't let me finish," I tell him, and he kisses me deep into the pillows.

"I changed my mind. I want to come inside you, not

your mouth."

"You can if you want," I tell him, and his eyes turn molten. "I'm on the pill, Vinny. I want to feel you inside me."

"With nothing between us," he adds, and I nod.

"Nothing between us."

Vinny kisses me, delving into my mouth and tangling his tongue with mine in a slow kiss that has my pussy throbbing and my hips tilting upward to try to get some friction.

Vinny pulls his hips back, and when I feel him press at my entrance, I moan, already loving the feeling of him.

"Look at me, baby. I want to see your eyes the first time I fuck you with nothing between us. I want to see how you feel." He pushes into me slowly, and I watch as his eyes turn to pools of chocolate that I'm drowning in.

"I see it all in your eyes, Lexi." He pushes in one final inch and presses his forehead to mine, kissing the corner of my mouth. "I love you," he whispers against my lips, and I choke on a sob.

"I love you too, Vinny."

Vinny kisses me hard and quick, then pulls back to look in my eyes. "Say it again."

"I love you," I whisper, smiling when he does. His eyes dart between mine, and I pull him back down to kiss me. "Now fuck me, Vincenzo. Show me you love me."

"Always, baby,"

Vinny fucks me slow at first, savoring the feel of us joining together.

In and out. In and out.

But when both of us needs more, Vinny quickens his

pace, and the pressure in me builds until I'm right on the edge.

"I can feel you're close, baby. Take me with you."

Thrusting into me even harder and faster, Vinny reaches between us and rubs my clit.

I cry out and pinch my eyes closed.

"No. Open. Let me see."

I find a way to peel my eyes open again and I see it all in his. I see his love, his desire, his need, his world. It's all there.

"Come with me, *dolcezza*." Vinny presses on my clit and I seize around him, arching off the bed and smashing my chest to his.

My throat closes around my scream and Vinny buries his face in my neck, groaning as he fills me with his release.

He kisses up my neck to my ear. "I love you."

"I love you," I whisper back, running my hands through his hair.

Vinny slides out of me and rolls us over so I'm on top of him. I lay my head on his chest and listen to his heart beating strongly beneath me.

We don't say anything else to each other for a stretch of time. We're just present in each other's space.

I trace random swirls on his chest. "I'm sorry I scared you," I start, and Vinny pauses his movements of twirling the ends of my hair around his finger. "I'm glad I have what I need to help my grandfather, but it was reckless, and I know I was lucky to make it out of there unscathed. I won't be taking a risk like that again."

He tugs on the ends of my hair. "Thank you."

I turn my head and prop my chin on top of the back of my hand to look up at him. Vinny grabs my ass and pulls me up him until my lips are hovering above his.

I grab his face and kiss him with a soft gentleness that has my core clenching and my heart twisting with love for him.

I press my forehead to his and smile. "Besides," I add playfully. "If I need money, I can just sit at a table in your casino and bleed you dry."

Laughing, he slaps my ass. "Do your worst, baby," he mumbles against my lips.

Rolling us back over, he kisses me until I lose my breath, and then he's sliding right back inside me, surprising me with the intrusion.

"Vinny!" I gasp, and he chuckles.

"Yeah, *dolcezza*. I need you again."

CHAPTER 33

Lexi

"How did you do this, Alexis?" nonno asks me, looking around the deli. It's been two weeks since it flooded and Lindsay made sure the work stayed on schedule.

Vinny comped nonno a room at The Aces while all the work was done, and he hadn't been back since the pipe burst, so I was able to keep it all under wraps.

"I took care of it, nonno. I wasn't going to have you give up when I know this is where you want to be. It's where I want to be, too. After I finish school, I'm going to work with you. If you don't mind, of course."

"Mind? Nothing would make me happier. I don't want to hold you back, though."

"You're not. Being here is what I love. But how about this? If I ever change my mind – which I know I won't – I promise to tell you."

"Deal." Nonno wraps me in my favorite hug and my heart soars. "I love you, Alexis. But I have one condition. You can't keep hovering and treating me like I'm going to keel over at any moment."

"Deal." I smile. "I'm just protective."

"As I am of you. Which I made sure to tell Vincenzo."

"Nonno!"

"What? That's my job."

"Thank you," I tell him gratefully. But the truth is, no one is more protective of me than Vinny, and I love it.

I met his family last weekend and he was in full protector mode. It made me nervous because I didn't know why he would have to protect me from his own family, but it all went well. They were nothing what I thought a family like theirs would be like, and I was welcomed like I was already a part of the family. And as someone with only two family members left, it was nice to be surrounded by a loud Italian family like I never had.

"Oh, I almost forgot! I have good news, nonno. Vinny told me last night that they arrested Eddie. He was pulled over for speeding in Pennsylvania and they saw he had warrants."

"Good. I'm glad he won't be able to hurt anyone else."

"Me too. And now that we can open again, we need to hire someone. Though, I insist on being involved in the process this time."

Nonno surprises me by agreeing. "I welcome your help. I clearly don't know how to pick a good employee."

"You gave someone a chance, nonno. That's never a bad thing. He just wasn't deserving of that chance, and he's paying for it now."

My phone starts ringing and I dig around in my purse for it. "You go look at everything and make sure you like it all. I have to take this."

I walk outside and answer it.

"Hey, sexy Lexi," Cassie says as soon as I pick up.

Laughing, I take a seat on one of the new benches. "Is this a new nickname for me? Because I kind of love it."

"You should tell Vinny that," she suggests.

"He already has a few names for me."

"I'll bet he does."

I pull my scarf tighter around my neck. "Did you call for a reason that doesn't involve discussing Vinny's sexy names for me?"

"I did." She laughs. "But if you tell me yours then I'll tell you mine."

"Tell me your what?"

"Nico's sexy names for me. We can see how original the brothers are."

"Cassie! You're with Nico? I thought he was just a little fun for a few days?"

"He was. He is. And I never said I was *with* him, but we can discuss this all later if we have a girl's night tonight. I feel like I haven't had quality Lexi time in forever."

"I'd love one!" I say excitedly. "Tonight, my place. I'll

make sure to have our favorites of everything ready."

"Yay! Okay, I'll see you later."

"I expect all the details of whatever's going on with you and Nico."

"We'll see," she says, and hangs up quickly before I can say anything else. But not to worry, I'll get it all out of her later.

The wind whips at my face and I tuck my chin down into my scarf and call Vinny.

"Hey, baby."

"Hi, *bello*. I have a question."

"What is it?"

"Did you know Cassie and Nico might be seeing each other?"

"No, I didn't. Did Cassie say that?"

"Well, yes and no. She said she's not with him, but I think they've been seeing each other."

"Is that a problem?"

"No. I just wanted to know if you knew. But I'll get it out of her tonight. We're having a girl's night. That's why I called. I hope you're not mad."

"Mad? Why would I be mad? Disappointed I won't have you in my arms tonight? Yes. But not mad. I'll be mad if this was the same kind of girl's night you told me you were having last time."

"No, this is a real one. I promise. But I'm going to miss you. I had a really long week and I stayed up all night last night to finish a paper. I could use a few orgasms so I'll pass out and sleep *very* well."

"Baby, don't tease me."

"Sorry." I smile. I love teasing him.

"Such a beautiful smile."

"How did you know I was smiling?" I look up and around, and smile wider when I see him walking towards me.

Hanging up, I run to him and he wraps his arms around me, lifting me up as I kiss him, loving the feel of his cold lips warming with mine.

"What are you doing here?" I ask when my feet are back on solid ground.

"I wouldn't miss the grand tour day."

"You're the best."

"Am I?" He grins. "Good to know."

"Well, come on. Let me give you a tour."

"And then we can go for a drive and I'll give you those orgasms so you can take a quick nap." He winks, and my core clenches.

"I need more than just a nap, Vinny, and I have class in a few hours."

"So, no orgasms?" He pouts.

"Not today." I lift up on my toes and kiss his cheek, then whisper in his ear, "But you know I love teasing you. When I see you tomorrow, I want you to get me naked and have your mouth on my pussy before you even say hi."

Vinny groans, pulling me tight against him. "That can be arranged. But we better get inside before I make good on that right here." He winks, tucking me under his arm.

CHAPTER 34
Vinny
3 months later...

Placing a fresh glass of champagne down on the table, I grip the back of Lexi's chair and lean in to kiss her cheek. "Dance with me, *dolcezza*," I whisper in her ear, and she smiles, taking a sip of champagne.

Gathering the bottom of her dress, she stands, and I take her hand. I walk us out onto the dance floor and pull her close, the slow song a perfect excuse to hold Lexi close in a room full of people.

Leo and Abri's wedding is one for the fucking books, and I've been dying to get my arms around my girl and feel the silk that's clinging to her curves for myself.

"Have I told you how beautiful you look tonight?"

"You have." She grins, her cheeks turning that pretty pink I love and her eyes shining with love. Of course, she's had a few drinks, so it could be that, but I'm going with love.

"Have I told you how handsome you look tonight?

"No, you haven't" I wink.

"You know I love you in your suits, but a tux?" She bites her lip. "Very sexy."

With my hands on her lower back, I rub my thumbs against her bare skin. "It's good to know what you'll be thinking when it's our wedding day and you're walking down the aisle towards me. That your soon-to-be husband is sexy as hell."

"What?" she breathes, her eyes wide and brilliantly blue.

Smiling at her look of surprise and confusion, I walk us off the dance floor and around the band to a set of French doors that lead to a balcony that overlooks the front of the property. The doors are hidden behind the curtain backdrop of the band, so no one else is out here to ruin this moment.

I walk her to the end and take her left hand, kissing the empty spot on her ring finger where a diamond will soon be sitting. "I said you were my wife the first night we met, so this is just one step closer to making it official."

Pulling the ring box from my pocket, I get down on one knee and Lexi's eyes water. "Vinny."

"Alexis Manzato, I love you. You're the best thing that's ever happened to me, and I want you by my side for the rest of my life. I want to be yours, and I want you to be mine forever. Will you marry me?"

"Vincenzo Carfano," she whispers, smiling down at me despite tears falling from her watery eyes. "I love you so damn much." She cups my cheek. "You're the best thing that's ever happened to me too, and nothing would make me happier than being your wife. Of course I'll marry you."

I open the ring box and her eyes widen at the gold band with a four-carat diamond sitting inside a simple setting.

"It's so big."

"That's something I'll never get tired of hearing." I wink, slipping the ring onto her finger. And the moment I do, the possessive asshole in me rears his ugly head.

Seeing my ring on her finger that tells the rest of the world she's mine, has my chest puffing with pride and my cock in need of staking his claim.

Lexi takes my face in her hands and bends down to kiss me. I wrap my arms around her and stand, keeping her crushed against me.

"Do you think anyone would notice if we snuck away for fifteen minutes? Twenty minutes? A half hour?"

"I wouldn't care if they did."

I walk her back inside to go in search of an empty room with a lock on the door. It shouldn't be hard.

I'll have to thank Leo for choosing to get married in a mansion with plenty of rooms to choose from.

We go up to the next level, and when I open the first door to see what kind of room it is, Lexi pushes me inside and closes the door behind us.

"Someone's eager," I say, and Lexi turns her back to me,

pulling her hair over her shoulder.

"Yes, I am. Now untie me. I don't want to ruin my dress."

"Anything you want, *dolcezza*." I kiss her bare shoulder and untie the silk string bow at her lower back. Loosening the ties, I push the thin straps off her shoulders and the entire dress falls to pool at her feet.

She steps out of it and I pick it up, draping it over one of the leather chairs in the study.

"I wouldn't want to ruin this masterpiece. It's my favorite color on you."

"That's why I chose it." She grins, that pretty pink stain that matches her dress blooming across her body as she stands before me naked.

"You've been naked this entire time?"

"Just for you, *bello*."

"Fuck, baby, you're perfect. But I think you'd be even more perfect bent over that couch."

She gives me one of her sweet smiles and does exactly that.

I groan. "Mhmm, I was right."

"Come fuck your fiancé, Vinny."

She's perfect.

She's fucking perfect.

And this view of her bent over for me with her pretty pink pussy on display and glistening for me is one I'll get to see for the rest of my life with her as my wife.

I'm the luckiest man in the world.

ABOUT THE AUTHOR

Rebecca is a dreamer through and through with permanent wanderlust. She has an endless list of places to go and see, hoping to one day experience the world and all it has to offer.

She's a Jersey girl who dreams of living in a place with freezing cold winters and lots of snow! When she's not writing, you can find her planning her next road trip and drinking copious amounts of coffee (preferably iced!).

newsletter, blog, shop, and links to all social media:
www.rebeccagannon.com

Follow me on Instagram to stay up-to-date on new releases, sales, teasers, giveaways, and so much more!
@rebeccagannon_author

Printed in Great Britain
by Amazon

43095475R00162